D0387270

A Wedding Vow from the Dark Side!

"You look lovely, my dear," the Imperial tyrant said, thrusting out his chest in military fashion. "And the moment you've secretly dreamed of for so long has now arrived. Princess Leia, you're about to become my bride!" Then he drew his right hand from behind his back, revealing a dozen black zinthorn flowers. "For you," he said. "A wedding bouquet!"

Without resisting, Leia accepted the horrible zinthorns. Then the grand moff, who was to perform the wedding ceremony, opened the Dark Book of Imperial Justice and began reading aloud. "We are witnesses to a momentous event," he began, "the marriage of our Imperial ruler to Princess Leia Organa, who shall now of her own free will renounce the Rebel Alliance and offer her eternal allegiance to the Dark Side! Thus, Leia will prepare herself to follow in the path of her father, Darth Vader, and at last become our queen!"

QUEEN OF THE EMPIRE

STAR WARS®

The Adventure Continues . . .

STAR WARS®

Book 5

QUEEN OF THE EMPIRE

PAUL DAVIDS
AND HOLLACE DAVIDS

Pencils by June Brigman
Finished Art by Karl Kesel

A BANTAM SKYLARK BOOK®
NEW YORK • TORONTO • LONDON • SYDNEY • AUCKLAND

RL 4, 008–012

QUEEN OF THE EMPIRE
A Bantam Skylark Book/March 1993

Skylark Books is a registered trademark of Bantam Books, a division of
Bantam Doubleday Dell Publishing Group, Inc. Registered in U.S.
Patent and Trademark Office and elsewhere.

Star Wars is a registered trademark of Lucasfilm Ltd.
All rights reserved. Used under authorization.

Cover art by Drew Struzan
Interior pencils by June Brigman
Finished interior art by Karl Kesel

All rights reserved.
Copyright © 1993 by Lucasfilm Ltd.

No part of this book may be reproduced or transmitted in any form or by
any means, electronic or mechanical, including photocopying,
recording, or by any information storage and retrieval system, without
permission in writing from the publisher.
For information address: Bantam Books.

If you purchased this book without a cover you should be aware that
this book is stolen property. It was reported as "unsold and destroyed"
to the publisher and neither the author nor the publisher has received
any payment for this "stripped book."

ISBN 0-553-15891-0

Published simultaneously in the United States and Canada

Bantam Books are published by Bantam Books, a division of Bantam Doubleday
Dell Publishing Group, Inc. Its trademark, consisting of the words "Bantam
Books" and the portrayal of a rooster, is Registered in U.S. Patent and Trademark
Office and in other countries. Marca Registrada. Bantam Books, 1540 Broadway,
New York, New York 10036.

PRINTED IN THE UNITED STATES OF AMERICA

OPM   19   18   17   16

In memory of George Pal,
Jedi Master of film fantasy,
whose inspiration shines as brightly
as the brilliant twin suns of Tatooine.

Acknowledgments

With thanks to George Lucas, the creator of Star Wars, to Lucy Wilson for her devoted guidance, to Charles Kochman for his unfailing insight, and to West End Games for their wonderful Star Wars sourcebooks— also to Betsy Gould, Peter Miller, and Richard A. Rosen for their advice and help.

LIBRARY
DEXTER SCHOOLS
DEXTER, NM 88230

$13.00

Bound / Perma Bound

3-21-02

The Rebel Alliance

Luke Skywalker

Princess Leia

Ken

Han Solo

Lando Calrissian

See-Threepio (C-3PO)

Baji

Fandar

The Empire

Trioculus

Grand Moff Hissa

Zorba the Hutt

Emdee-Five (MD-5)

Grand Moff Muzzer

Tibor

Supreme Prophet Kadann

Triclops

A long time ago,
in a galaxy
far, far away...

The Adventure Continues . . .

It was an era of darkness, a time when the evil Empire ruled the galaxy. Fear and terror spread across every planet and moon as the Empire tried to crush all who resisted—but still the Rebel Alliance survived.

The headquarters of the Alliance Senate are located in a cluster of ancient temples hidden within the rain forest on the fourth moon of Yavin. It was the senate that now led the valiant fight to establish a new galactic government, and to restore freedom and justice to the galaxy. In pursuit of this quest, Mon Mothma, the Rebel Alliance leader, organized the Senate Planetary Intelligence Network, also known as SPIN.

SPIN conducts its perilous missions with the help of Luke Skywalker and his pair of droids known as See-Threepio (C-3PO) and Artoo-Detoo (R2-D2). Other members of SPIN include the beautiful Princess Leia; Han Solo, the dashing pilot of the spaceship *Millennium Falcon;* Han's copilot Chewbacca, a hairy alien Wookiee; and Lando Calrissian, the former governor of Cloud City on the planet Bespin.

Lando Calrissian had been forced to abandon his post in Cloud City after gambling away his position to Zorba the Hutt, a sluglike alien who is the father of the deceased gangster, Jabba the Hutt. Having learned about his son's death at the hands of Princess Leia, Zorba now seeks revenge against Leia and the Rebel Alliance. Princess Leia and her brother Luke Skywalker, the last of the Jedi Knights, have managed to elude the wrath of the Hutt—at least for the time being.

The Jedi Knights, an ancient society of brave and noble warriors, believed that victory comes not just from physical strength but from a mysterious power called the Force. The Force lies hidden deep within all things. It has two sides, one side that can be used for good, the other side a power of absolute evil.

Guided by the Force, and by the spirit of his first Jedi teacher, Obi-Wan Kenobi, Luke Skywalker was led to the legendary Lost City of the Jedi. Deep underground on the fourth moon of Yavin, the Lost City proved to be the home of a boy named Ken, said to be a Jedi Prince. Ken had no human friends and had never before left the Lost City to journey above ground. He knew nothing of his origins and had been raised from early childhood by a loyal group of caretaker droids who had once served the ancient Jedi Knights. Ken has since left the underground city and joined Luke and the Rebel Alliance.

With the Empire's evil leaders, Emperor Palpatine and Darth Vader, now destroyed, a new era has begun. Kadann, the Supreme Prophet of the Dark Side, foretold that a new Emperor would arise, and on his hand he would wear an indestructible symbol of evil—the glove of Darth Vader!

Three-eyed Trioculus, the former Supreme Slavelord of the spice mines of Kessel, falsely claimed that he was Emperor Palpatine's son. With help from the Imperial grand moffs, who aided Trioculus in his rise to power so they could all share the rule of the Empire, Trioculus succeeded in finding Darth Vader's glove, thus fulfilling Kadann's prophecy. However, the Emperor's real three-eyed son, Triclops, has long been a secret prisoner of the Empire, locked away in Imperial insane asylums most of his life. For some mysterious reason the Empire fears him, still keeping him alive, while denying his very existence.

Knowing that Trioculus was neither Emperor Palpatine's real son nor a true master of the Dark Side, Kadann warned Trioculus that he must locate the Lost City of the Jedi and destroy a certain Jedi Prince. This prince, Ken, had learned many dark and dangerous Imperial secrets from the droids of the Lost City. The information, if revealed, could threaten Trioculus's reign as Emperor, and bring it to a sudden and tragic end.

Despite his efforts, Trioculus failed to locate the Lost City, or the young Jedi Prince. He then made the mistake of falling in love with Princess Leia.

When Zorba the Hutt learned that Trioculus wanted to protect Princess Leia, preventing him from taking revenge upon her, Zorba became furious. He took Trioculus prisoner and encased him in carbonite, freezing him in suspended animation and displaying the carbonized block in the Cloud City Museum as a living statue.

The Imperial grand moffs were sent on a mission to recover the carbonized body of Trioculus from the Cloud City Museum, but Kadann seized the carbonite block from them and vaporized it with neutron beams, pronouncing himself the new leader of the Galactic Empire.

On the Alliance's last mission, Luke Skywalker came upon Emperor Palpatine's real three-eyed son, Triclops, on the planet Duro. Luke helped Triclops escape from Imperial control, then brought him back to Mount Yoda. It was then revealed that the Empire considered Triclops insane because he passionately believed in peace and disarmament—and planned to destroy his father's evil Empire.

The Rebel Alliance continues its struggle to restore freedom and justice to the galaxy. A new Alliance military center has been built atop Mount Yoda on the planet Dagobah, the swampy world where the Jedi Master Yoda lived. This well-guarded fortress is called DRAPAC—the Defense Research and Planetary Assistance Center. There Princess Leia is stationed, unaware that powerful Imperial forces are underway to reshape her destiny, intent upon turning her to the Dark Side and making her—the Queen of the Empire!

CHAPTER 1
Project Decoy

"Project Decoy is ready for testing. There will be an experimental demonstration at 2200." Fandar, the flappy-eared, flat-nosed Chadra-Fan alien scientist, transmitted his top secret message from an Alliance laboratory deep inside Mount Yoda on the planet Dagobah.

Mon Mothma, leader of the Rebel Alliance, received Fandar's message in her office at the Rebel fortress known as DRAPAC, the Defense Research and Planetary Assistance Center. DRAPAC was located at the peak of Mount Yoda, and served as the Alliance's newest military installation. Mon Mothma promptly summoned the group that would accompany her to the demonstration. The group included Princess Leia, Luke Skywalker, Han Solo, and at Luke's suggestion, Ken, the twelve-year-old Jedi Prince.

One by one they stepped inside the tubular transport that led down to the secret labs of DRAPAC. "Authorization to descend to Restricted Sublevel D-13," Mon Mothma said, waving her hand over a small blinking security device.

They grasped the handrails and traveled downward until they reached the thirteenth underground level. Then they passed through several security checks—through barred gates, thick doors guarded by armed droids, and a machine that tested their biorhythmic vibrations to double-check their identities—and finally through an entrance marked PROJECT DECOY.

"Fugo and I are pleased all of you could join us on such short notice," Fandar said, raising his long-fingered hand in greeting.

Fandar and Fugo were scientists of the Chadra-Fan species from the planet Chad. Chadra-Fan are small, quick-witted creatures resembling rodents. The combination of their infrared sight, hypersensitive sense of smell, and keen hearing makes the Chadra-Fan physically and mentally perceptive creatures.

Fugo turned his beady black eyes at Ken in a look of surprise. "I didn't realize that a boy your age could have security clearance to enter here."

"Age isn't the deciding factor in Ken's case," Luke Skywalker replied, knitting his brow.

"Luke is quite right," Mon Mothma confirmed. "Ken was raised in the Lost City of the Jedi. He's had access to the master Jedi computer in the Jedi Library, which contains many invaluable secrets about the Empire."

"Then we welcome you here, Ken," Fandar said, raising his flappy ears. He then turned and pointed to a metal barrier that concealed part of the room. "We are gathered here to share a special moment with Princess Leia," Fandar said with a smile. "Princess Leia, here's the result of the project you helped us with. Meet Princess Leia Organa II."

Leia was overcome with surprise as a woman

stepped out from behind a metal barrier. The woman was a lifelike duplicate of Leia—an almost-identical-looking twin!

"I know we all like to feel unique," the other Leia said, "but life can be full of surprises."

"Who *is* that lady?" Ken asked, blinking in disbelief as he glanced from one Leia to the other.

"I'm the newest member of SPIN, stationed here at DRAPAC," the second Leia said.

"She's what we call a Human Replica Droid," Fandar explained.

"You're a droid?" Ken gasped.

"This is really creepy," Han said.

"It's fantastic!" Luke exclaimed. "Leia, she looks just like you. She even talks like you. Her smile is the same as yours, and so are her gestures."

"Fandar and Fugo, you two certainly did a good job," Leia commented.

"This droid will be used as a decoy for Princess Leia when she's out on dangerous missions," Mon Mothma explained. "That's how Project Decoy got its name."

"Now for the next part of our demonstration," Fandar began. "If you'll all join me behind this transparent shield."

Fandar reached into his lab desk and took out a floating orb about the size of his fist. He tossed the mechanical ball into the air, and the device sailed to the other side of the protective screen.

As the floating orb approached the Human Replica Droid of Leia, her lifelike eyes suddenly turned bright green. A high-energy laser beam shot out of each eye, causing the mechanical orb to explode.

KABOOOOM!

Metal fragments smashed against the transparent screen that protected the witnesses.

Fandar reached into his pocket and took out a small coin, then flipped it into the air. The Human Replica Droid's eyes turned green again as laser beams once again shot out of her pupils.

But they misfired! Instead of burning a hole in the coin, the lasers burned a small hole in the transparent screen, hitting Fandar's chest, and striking his left heart.

"Oh no!" Ken shouted. "What happened? What went wrong?"

Clear, thin blood began pumping out of Fandar's side, dripping down his DRAPAC uniform. Gasping, he lost his balance and fell headfirst to the floor of his laboratory. Fugo rushed over at once to help Fandar.

Leia reached for a medical aid unit that was mounted on the wall. Without wasting a moment, she used a medical crystallizer instrument to stop the flow of blood.

"Ken, do you know how to find Baji?" Luke asked.

"Last I saw Baji," the boy replied, "Threepio was helping him water plants in the north tower."

Luke contacted his golden droid, See-Threepio, in the north DRAPAC tower, summoning both him and Baji at once to help with a medical emergency.

While Leia, Fugo, and the others continued to care for the wounded Chadra-Fan scientist, Threepio

entered Baji's greenhouse and called out to the healer, who was a specialist in herbal medicines. "Oh dear, oh my, Master Luke says we must hurry!" Threepio exclaimed to Baji, who was kneeling to plant some very rare seedlings.

Luke had met Baji, a nine-foot-tall Ho'Din alien from the planet Moltok, during Luke's quest for the Lost City of the Jedi. Baji was then captured by Imperials and forced to join the Imperial medical staff. Fortunately, however, Baji had been rescued during an Alliance attack on an Imperial command center. Now the Ho'Din alien lived a very simple, quiet life at the Mount Yoda fortress, tending his greenhouse of medicinal plants, rare herbs, and flowers.

All security checks between the north tower and Sublevel D-13 were temporarily suspended, in order to permit Threepio and Baji immediate access to Fandar's lab.

Baji examined the patient. Then he said:

"Fandar's right heart pumps on
But his left one is nearly gone
Transplant another heart with no delays
Or death shall come in just three days."

"We'll need a heart donor then," Fugo said. "But I'm the only other Chadra-Fan here on Dagobah. I would gladly sacrifice my own life for Fandar, but—"

Interrupting, Mon Mothma turned to Han and asked, "Can the *Millennium Falcon* still make it to Chad in twenty-five standard time parts?" she asked.

"Less time than that, probably," Han replied.

"Ever since the mechanics at Orbiting Shipyard Alpha installed a new Carbanti 29L electromagnetic package, the *Falcon*'s been flying like a dream."

"Good—it's up to you to get Fandar back to Chad as fast as you can," Mon Mothma instructed. "Take him to the heart transplant center at Chadra-Fan Hospital."

"I'm going with you, Han," Leia said.

"We'll take See-Threepio and Artoo-Detoo along with us," Luke offered. "Threepio will make an excellent caretaker for Fandar while he recovers from his operation. And Artoo will be a reliable copilot."

"A very constructive idea, Master Luke," Threepio chimed in.

"Han and Leia can handle this on their own, Luke," Mon Mothma interjected. "I have a serious matter here that requires your assistance—and Chewbacca's too."

"You mean the problem with Triclops?"

"A perceptive guess," Mon Mothma replied. She then turned her attention to Fandar's injury, avoiding further discussion of Triclops.

Piloted by Han Solo and copiloted by Princess Leia, the *Millennium Falcon* blasted off with See-Threepio and Artoo-Detoo, departing the swampy world where the great Jedi Master, Yoda, had trained Luke Skywalker in the ways of the Jedi Knights. The spaceship proceeded beyond the Dagobah star system, swerved around a massive asteroid belt, and plunged through a region that was filled with swirling space gas caused by a supernova explosion thousands of years ago. Then the *Falcon* made the jump to hyperspace, zooming off at faster-than-light speed.

Twenty-two standard time parts later, as the spaceship decelerated, the blue-white sun of planet Chad came into view. Han and Leia could see Chad off in the distance, with its nine small moons appearing as tiny specks of light.

"Look, Han," Princess Leia said, "the entire planet seems to be covered by thick clouds."

"Huge storm system, Princess," Han explained. "Happens all the time here now. And they've got no one to blame but themselves."

"How so?"

"It's because of the Lactils. They've got so many of those smelly milk-producing creatures on this planet, the situation is now totally out of control." Han checked his Navicomputer to figure out the best angle for the *Millennium Falcon*'s approach. "It may be good for Chad, from a business point of view, that they're now the dairy capital of the galaxy, but no one ever stopped to consider that Lactils exhale enormous quantities of methane gas. And too much methane is bad news for the upper atmosphere."

"*Tzchlootle!*" beeped the little barrel-shaped droid, Artoo-Detoo. "*Bzing-zooch, PZEEep badoing!*"

"Goodness," Threepio translated, "Artoo has made a startling calculation using advanced spectrographic analysis. He's concluded that so much methane gas has polluted the upper atmosphere, it's caused a terrible greenhouse effect on Chad. The planet is overheated, consequently warming up the seas—and

warm oceans give rise to violent hurricanes."

"Like the one looming over the region of Chadra-Fan Hospital right now," Han said, taking a reading on his monitor.

"Threepio, go check up on Fandar," Leia said. "As we land in the storm, you may have to adjust the force field that's keeping him afloat."

"Oh dear, oh my, force-field adjustment coming right up," Threepio fretted.

"I hope you're ready for this, Leia," Han said, as he began the descent into the turbulent atmosphere. "I'd rather face an armada of Imperial starfighters than try to land in a hurricane this bad. But here goes nothing—"

The gale-force winds stretched all the way into the upper atmosphere.

SHWOOOOOOOOOSH!

The winds tore at the *Falcon*, ripping at its outer surfaces, as Threepio departed the cockpit to check up on Fandar.

KRAKKKK!

"There goes the passive sensor antenna for our microwave radio," Han said in dismay.

ROOOOOOAAAAAAR!

"Sounds like we just lost our escape pod!" Leia concluded, grimacing.

Han glanced out the window, peering through the torrential rains and black clouds, quickly confirming Leia's suspicion. Han winced, remembering how much it had cost to repair the *Millennium Falcon* on their last mission from Mount Yoda.

Threepio was knocked around relentlessly as he tried to look after Fandar. "Oh my. If you can't fly any better than this, Han Solo, they should suspend your pilot's license," Threepio complained, well aware that Han was some distance away in the cockpit and couldn't possibly hear him.

And then came the sharp sound of crunching metal.

"Oh goodness!" Threepio said with alarm. "I've got a dent in my right forearm! And I was just replated too!"

The *Falcon* was tossed around like a bottle on the sea, as Han tried to maneuver it through the ferocious storm clouds. Lightning pounded the ship, shorting out its main lights. The inside of the *Falcon* suddenly went black, and the temperature began to drop. "Terrific," Han said sarcastically. "If our thermal amplifier is down, this cockpit is going to get colder than the spice mines of Kessel. But so help me, I'm going to land this baby in one piece, or I'm nothing but a Kowakian monkey-lizard."

Han blinked, his eyes adjusting to the darkened cockpit, where the only light came from the faint, colored dials and buttons on the navigation console. Then he navigated the *Falcon* toward the eye of the storm, fighting the awesome power of the hurricane's winds all the way.

CHAPTER 2
Rockslide on Chad

Chadra-Fan Hospital was perched on a low bluff overlooking the pounding waves of the shore. Looming high above were towering cliffs. The hospital was being drenched by the hardest rainfall Han had ever seen, flooding the ground outside the spaceship hangars, which were connected to the medical building by long corridors.

Han, Leia, and the droids stepped down the ramp of the *Falcon* and into a hangar, relieved to be on solid ground once again.

"Well, another safe landing from the galaxy's best Corellian pilot," Han said boastfully. "And you can thank my unfailing triple combination—daredevil skill, blind luck, and a little trust in the Force."

"A *little* trust in the Force? Personally, I have a *lot* of trust in the Force," Leia replied. Like her brother, Luke Skywalker, Leia was also a Jedi, and therefore understood the power of the Force far better than Han. "If you ask me, that's what got us here in one piece—not your daredevil skill and blind luck."

"You two may have arrived in one piece," Threepio complained, "but just look at *me*. My poor dented arm! I certainly hope we can get to a Droid Repair Shop soon."

The four of them were greeted in the hangar by several furry Chadra-Fan who helped Han transport

Fandar on his floating stretcher. The cot hung suspended in midair by the force of miniature repulsorlifts on the underside. Artoo-Detoo managed to roll along beside Han without any problems, but Leia and Threepio were stopped in their tracks by a suspicious and quarrelsome guard. The guard demanded to know how Fandar had been injured. Caught up in the urgency of getting the wounded Chadra-Fan to the heart transplant center, Han and Artoo didn't notice that Leia and Threepio were being detained.

The hurricane continued in all its fury, as Han Solo, Artoo-Detoo, and Fandar arrived at the operating room.

Artoo plugged himself into the medical monitoring equipment, so he could keep track of Fandar's vital signs during the operation. Meanwhile, the team of surgeons, led by Chief Chan, located a suitable replacement heart in their cryogenic storage room containing organs for transplant. As they commenced the operation, lightning suddenly struck the hospital's domed power core. A jolt surged into the monitoring machines, sizzling several of Artoo's electrical circuits.

"Buu-bee-oowwwbzeee-bjEEEch!" Artoo screeched as he rolled out of the operating room and into the hallway.

"What's your problem?" Han asked, chasing after the droid. But Artoo kept rolling away, veering left and right like a drunken alien on hover skates. When Han finally caught up with the barrel-shaped droid, Artoo spun in circles and then fell over.

"Don't tell me that the lightning fried your circuits, Artoo. We don't have time to repair you now.

Besides—" Han stopped in the middle of his sentence and glanced around with concern. "Now where in the world do you suppose Leia went?"

Another bolt of lightning hit nearby, this one striking an outcrop of rocks on one of the cliffs towering above the hospital. The resulting landslide thundered and rumbled with fearsome force.

Then the roof above the corridor tore open and collapsed, as tons of rocks poured down around Han and Artoo, trapping them beneath the rubble.

Diplomat that she was, Leia poured on her charm, convincing the guard at the Chadra-Fan hangar that she had come with Fandar to help.

Leia and See-Threepio were released by the guard—just in time to witness the rockslide bury the corridor—and Han and Artoo with it.

At first Leia thought Han must surely be dead. Turning pale from shock, she took a deep breath and tried to calm herself, putting herself in touch with the Force.

Han was still alive—she knew it! There was still hope. But how could she get Han and Artoo out from under all those rocks?

In desperation, Leia and Threepio hurried back to the guard at the hangar and shouted for help. "This is an emergency!" she shouted. "We need a Boulder-Dozer right away! Please help us!"

Boulder-Dozers were equipped with powerful laser-scorchers, especially designed to vaporize debris and cut holes through solid rocks.

"We have several in the storage building by the equipment yard," the guard said, leading the way.

The guard opened a wide emergency exit door. As they headed out of the hangar and toward the equipment yard, the horrendous winds practically blew them off their feet.

"We've got to hurry!" Leia shouted.

The guard unlocked a warehouse door, and Princess Leia hopped aboard the first Boulder-Dozer she saw. She flipped the power switch, but nothing happened.

"Looks like the rain has flooded the Nebulon starter unit," Leia declared.

"We've never had any trouble with it before," the guard said. "It's a top-of-the-line Rendili Boulder-Dozer with a Navicomputer control."

"Perhaps I can help," Threepio volunteered. "I once came in contact with a Corellian engineer who worked for the Rendili Vehicle Corporation. Whenever one of *his* Boulder-Dozers failed to start, he crawled underneath it like this and pushed the power modulation lever back and forth a few times—"

VRRRRRROOOOM!

"Good work, Threepio!" Leia exclaimed, and then thanked the guard for his help.

Threepio climbed aboard the Boulder-Dozer and Leia took off, driving at full speed through the pouring rain. She reentered the hangar at the emergency exit, then continued into the corridor that led to the hospital.

Arriving at the area where Han and Artoo were trapped, Princess Leia aimed the Boulder-Dozer's laser-scorchers at the pile of rubble that had fallen through the roof. Then she turned the lasers on full blast, vaporizing the solid rock to create a large hole.

TSSSSSST!

Realizing that Han Solo's life depended upon her success, Leia felt a choking, stinging sensation build up in her throat. When the inside of the hole glowed bright red, Leia shut down the laser-scorch-

ers. She knew that if she cut too quickly through the rubble, the laser's beams might hit Han and Artoo, vaporizing them as well!

As the last few lavalike chunks of rock vaporized, to her relief Leia could see that Han was all right, apparently without any broken bones.

"Quick thinking, Princess!" Han shouted excitedly. "But it's hotter than a steam bath in here right now!"

"That's from the laser-scorchers," she said. "Wait for the rocks to cool down first before you crawl out."

When the inside of the hole changed from a fiery bright red to steely gray, Han crawled through the opening on his hands and knees, his face and clothes grimy, sweat dripping down his cheeks.

"I don't recommend that experience," Han said, brushing himself off. He sighed and wiped his brow. "You know, Leia, I thought I'd seen you for the last time. And, well—" He paused, searching for the right words.

"Well what?" she asked.

"That would have been a shame," Han admitted.

"I'll agree with that."

"A *big* shame," he added. "All my plans for us were almost crushed by those rocks."

Leia's eyebrows raised questioningly. "*What* plans for us, Han?"

Han glanced away. "Hey, a Rendili Navi-computer-controlled Boulder-Dozer!" he exclaimed excitedly, quickly changing the subject. "Made by the good ol' Corellian Engineering Corporation. I'll have to thank them."

"You could try thanking *me* first," Leia said.

"Sorry, Princess," Han replied, embarrassed. "Thanks for saving my life. Thanks a lot."

"*Bzooooch gneeeech!*" Artoo-Detoo interrupted. The little droid was still trapped beneath the rubble.

"Artoo's circuits went haywire when he plugged himself into the medical monitor—there was some kind of electrical malfunction from all the lightning. We're going to have to get him serviced."

"*Fzzzwoooop bzeeeedle squuAAAAAk!*" Artoo tooted frantically.

"Fuss fuss!" See-Threepio said, reacting to the noisy barrel-shaped droid. "Honestly, you screech more than a squirmy Ranat!"

The golden droid climbed through the hole in the rubble that the laser-scorchers had burned. "As if it wasn't enough that I've dented an arm already on this trip!" Threepio complained. "By the time I get you out from behind these rocks, I'll need *two* new arms—and a complete replating to get rid of my scratches!"

CHAPTER 3
Han Solo's Big Plans

Luke Skywalker leaned forward anxiously in the small lab room in DRAPAC's south tower, staring through a two-way mirror. Triclops, now sleeping restlessly in a barren room with one floating mattress, was beginning to mumble something about his father, the evil Emperor Palpatine.

Luke listened intently, realizing the importance of this strange, haggard man with a third eye at the back of his head. Luke, Ken, and Chewbacca were monitoring him carefully. They knew full well that Triclops would have been recognized by the Imperials as the legal heir to the Empire if he hadn't been such an outspoken supporter of peace and disarmament. But that fact had forced the Imperials to keep Triclops's existence a secret, and they sentenced him to life in the Imperial Reprogramming Institute and Imperial insane asylums.

Luke was aware that he had taken a risk by trusting Triclops and bringing him to their Alliance fortress. And Mon Mothma was now becoming increasingly suspicious that Triclops might turn out to be an Imperial spy. Triclops had done nothing consciously to earn their distrust. But his behavior while he was asleep was extremely suspect. At times Triclops flew into fits of rage while he slept—even Chewbacca, strong as the Wookiee was, had trouble restraining Triclops during those outbursts.

Ken had made quite a few discoveries about Triclops from the master Jedi computer in the Jedi Library—information that Ken felt was important for Luke and the Alliance to understand. The droids of the Lost City had never permitted Ken to see *all* their secret files on Triclops. But the information Ken *had* seen convinced him that the Empire kept Triclops alive for a very specific reason—otherwise Triclops would have been executed by those who were loyal to the Dark Side long ago.

"When Triclops is awake, he never remembers his evil dreams," Ken explained. "As you now know, Triclops talks in his sleep. And his dreams are the reason the Empire has kept him alive all these years, rather than sentencing him to death."

"What exactly do you know about his dreams?" Luke asked.

"All I know," Ken said, "is that sometimes Triclops dreams up plans for new weapons and deadly war machines. He gives the specifications in his sleep, and the Empire manufactures them. Triclops doesn't even know he invents anything at all, let alone *what* he invents. He's like two people living inside the same body—part of him good and well-intentioned; the other part an evil and dangerous genius inventor."

Triclops, who had wild white hair and scars on his temples from all the electroshock therapy the Empire had given him, tossed in his sleep and began speaking again. Luke, Ken, and Chewbacca listened

carefully to his every word.

"It won't work unless you use . . . a powerful miniunit that's much more than a stun projectile," Triclops said in a low, distant voice. "It should have a laser power equal to . . . equal to the Atgar 1.4, capable of functioning at all temperatures. Controlled by an active sensor package and . . . and a tactical display with extended range. Variable sensor rate 55, blast radius of 20-plus, v-150 ionization. Then the eyes will work."

That was all Triclops said as his fitful dream ended.

Luke studied Triclops's message, and at daybreak he and Ken shared the message with Fugo in the Project Decoy lab on Sublevel D-13.

When the Chadra-Fan scientist heard the words "Atgar 1.4," his two hearts started beating rapidly.

And when Fugo heard that Triclops had said, "Variable sensor rate 55 with a blast radius of 20-plus," he gasped, and his large ears flapped excitedly.

"It's a feat of mind reading that's absolutely *impossible!*" Fugo explained to Luke and Ken. "Either that, or we have a serious security leak here at DRAPAC. How could Triclops, whom I have never even met, know that just yesterday I modified our Princess Leia Human Replica Droid to give her eyes a laser power equal to an Atgar 1.4 Imperial Antivehicle Laser Cannon? And how could he know," Fugo continued, "that the reason Fandar was wounded was because we built the droid's eyes with the wrong sensor rate and incorrect blast radius?"

"Remarkable," Luke Skywalker said, shaking his

head in amazement.

"The sensor rate we needed was 55—exactly what Triclops said," Fugo continued, "and the 20-plus blast radius with a v-150 ionization is probably correct as well. I will test that information immediately."

"Perhaps Triclops has mind-reading powers that are similar to Jedi abilities," Ken concluded.

"Or perhaps his sleeping mind is so powerful," Luke speculated, "that he can mind read the thoughts and military secrets of everyone working here at Mount Yoda. And if that's true, he could prove very dangerous indeed."

On Chad the last of the storm clouds departed, and the planet's nine glowing moons lit up the heavens in splendor. Chief Chan examined Fandar and announced that his heart transplant operation was a success. However, Fandar would have to remain on Chad for the foreseeable future, in order to continue his recovery at the Chadra-Fan Hospital. Under these circumstances, there was no reason for Han, Leia, See-Threepio, and Artoo-Detoo to delay their departure any further. After having spent two days on Chad already, the four emissaries of the Alliance bid the Chadra-Fan farewell and reboarded the *Millennium Falcon*.

Once they were all seated inside the navigation room of the spaceship and prepared for takeoff, co-pilot Princess Leia said, "Next stop, Dagobah!"

"Wrong," Han said. "Next stop, Hologram Fun World!"

Thrilling images of the most spectacular space

station in the galaxy filled Leia's mind—a fun park where hologram experiences seemed to make every wish come true.

"We can't go to Hologram Fun World, Han," Leia protested. "We've got work to do for SPIN back at Mount Yoda. We don't have time to waste."

"Who said we were going to waste time?" Han said. And then, just like that, he blurted out, "We're going to elope!"

"Wha . . . what?" Princess Leia stammered.

"Well, uhm, it's just that, uhm . . ."

"Are you asking me to marry you, Han?" Leia asked.

"I guess you could look at it that way, if you want," Han replied. "I mean, that's what it usually means to elope, doesn't it? To fly off somewhere in a hurry and get, and get, you know . . ."

Leia was speechless.

Han gave a deep sigh and continued, "Don't act as if this comes as such a big shock, okay? I told you when you saved my life that all my plans for us were almost crushed by those rocks. That just started me thinking, I guess."

"Thinking about me?" Leia asked.

"Thinking about the fact that I'm not getting any younger, and that if I ever want any pip-squeak Solo kids running around my sky house tugging at my boots, well, it just wouldn't seem right unless you were their mother." Han gazed into her eyes. "Does that make any sense?"

"Perfect sense," she answered.

As Han took Princess Leia in his arms to kiss her, Threepio glanced away in the opposite direction.

"Gracious!" the droid exclaimed. "Why do humans get so sentimental—it simply boggles my brain circuits!"

Threepio covered his eye sensors with his metal hands so he wouldn't have to look, but he did peek every few moments to see if Han and Leia were done embracing. As a protocol droid, a specialist in droid-human relations, Threepio knew he should be able to tolerate it when humans became affectionate. But still, to Threepio, kissing seemed a silly and unnecessary act.

"Do you have any objections to our getting married, Princess?" Han asked. "Speak now or forever hold your peace."

"Of course I don't have any objections," she said, "except—"

As Leia stopped in midsentence, Han glanced at her suspiciously. "Except what?"

"I always dreamed of a big wedding, and wear-

ing a beautiful white wedding dress with a long train. I imagined Luke would be there to give me away, and all our friends would join us in dancing, and there would be a huge feast, and—"

"Why it'd take months to plan a wedding like that," Han said with a slight frown. "Who knows what could happen to us between now and then? Besides, we can always have a party with our friends later on. We could celebrate our getting hitched when we have more time."

Leia's eyes brightened. "You know, come to think of it, it might actually be thrilling to elope. Nobody would ever expect it of us!"

Han smiled. "What do you droids say?" he asked.

"Tzoooooch!" Artoo beeped. *"Dweeeboo bzoooch!"*

"Artoo says it's a fine idea. Besides, he's always wanted to see Hologram Fun World," Threepio translated. "As for me, I agree, you two *should* get married. It's about time. I mean . . . I've never been to a space station amusement park before—they say there's a first time for everything!"

Han smiled and gave Princess Leia a wink. Little did she know that right under the navigation console was a small drawer that contained a sparkling ring Han planned to give her—an ancient ring that belonged to a Corellian princess long, long ago. It was given to Han by a Duro archaeologist named Dustangle on Han's last mission from Mount Yoda. Little did he think at the time that he would have the nerve to use it.

Soon they would be at Hologram Fun World together. The amusement park was located inside a dome that floated in a helium gas cloud near the Zabian star system. There, they could live every fantasy they had ever had, from waterskiing off the edge of a thousand-foot waterfall, to surfboarding on a river of burning lava.

The *Millennium Falcon* left Chad and its nine moons far behind as Han shifted his spaceship into hyperdrive and set out for the one place in the galaxy where *anything* could happen—and almost always did!

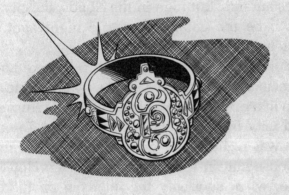

CHAPTER 4
Hologram Fun World

Cloud City on the planet Bespin was usually a blur of tourist activities—skysailing, sightseeing in cloud cars, gambling in casinos, dancing, and dining in fine floating restaurants. But high in the clouds, the city that used to be the galaxy's favorite night spot was strangely quiet.

Zorba the Hutt, who had replaced Lando Calrissian as Governor of Cloud City after defeating Lando in a card game of sabacc, had just returned to Cloud City from a voyage to the planet Tatooine. Zorba was reclining for an afternoon snooze in the penthouse suite inside his Holiday Towers Hotel and Casino, when suddenly the intercom on his desk made a loud noise.

BZZZZZZ!

"Who dares disturb my afternoon nap?" Zorba snarled.

"It's Checksum, the audit droid, and my assistant," came the reply. "We have an appointment."

The Hutt suddenly recalled that he *did* have a very important appointment with a group of hotel business droids to receive his monthly accounting. Zorba permitted his droid guests to enter, then shut off his intercom so he wouldn't be disturbed.

"Losses to the Holiday Towers Hotel and Casino for this past month equal 18,545,372 credits," Checksum said, "including losses from empty hotel rooms, and unsold restaurant food."

"That's outrageous!" Zorba fumed, pounding his right fist into his left hand. "My hotel and casino has always turned a profit before. Why has business gone bad here in Cloud City?"

"For the answer to that question," Checksum said, "I refer you to Debit-101, our audit droid specialist in business strategies. Debit, your analysis?"

"Certainly," the business analyst droid replied. "It appears Cloud City faces terrible competition from Hologram Fun World. Our studies show that most tourists would prefer to experience hologram adventures," Debit-101 continued, "rather than to risk losing credits gambling in Cloud City casinos. Another reason perhaps—Hologram Fun World doesn't have a bad crime problem like you have here in Cloud City."

Zorba scowled, getting so mad that he struck Debit-101 with his stubby right arm. He then pounded Checksum with his left fist, sending both droids clattering to the floor.

An hour later, Zorba called before him all the best bounty hunters in Cloud City.

"You will come with me to Hologram Fun World to terrorize the guests, rob the banks, take entertainers as hostages, and destroy the hologram rides," Zorba the Hutt announced. "By the time we're done with Hologram Fun World, a tourist would be a fool to even *think* of taking a vacation there."

Confident that he had figured out the way to increase business back in Cloud City once again, Zorba took off in his wheezing old spaceship, the *Zorba Express*.

The bounty hunters, led by Tibor the Barabel, flew in an armada of spaceships close behind.

Han Solo pointed to the glowing, transparent dome floating in the center of a blue cloud of helium gas. "Feast your eyes on Hologram Fun World," he said, "where a few short hours from now we'll become husband and wife."

"I beg your pardon," Leia replied. "You mean, 'where a few short hours from now we'll become *bride and groom*.'"

"Same difference," Han insisted.

"Hardly," Leia replied. "*Husband and wife* implies that the masculine gender belongs in first position, whereas *bride and groom*—"

"Fine, all right, no problem," Han interrupted with a smile, "if 'bride and groom' makes the princess happy, then have it your way. Like they say, 'ladies first' and all that."

"Exactly," Leia said, smiling.

From her seat in the cockpit of the *Millennium Falcon*, Princess Leia gazed at the glittering yellow-green dome, surrounded by waves of rippling color. They were fast approaching. "It's too bad Ken's not here with us," she said. "I'm sure he would have a great time."

"Luke would love Hologram Fun World too," Han replied. "He's always wanted to go hover-skiing down the side of an exploding volcano."

"I certainly hope they've got a well-equipped Droid Repair Shop there," Threepio interjected. "It was quite distressing that the one back on Chad was closed due to storm damage."

"Hologram Fun World has the best service center for droids in this part of the galaxy," Han replied.

"*BzEEEt GliiiiipzEEp!*" Artoo tooted.

"Yes, Artoo, we were fortunate indeed that the hangar mechanic was able to temporarily readjust your circuits," Threepio responded impatiently.

Han decelerated the *Falcon*, coasting slowly toward their destination. As they descended, they passed a gigantic neon sign that greeted visitors with the words: A WORLD OF DREAMS COME TRUE!

Inside the dome, Leia could see fantastic fire-

works exploding high above the rides and attractions, bursting in showers of brilliant sparks.

Leia stared at the winding slide ramps for the ride called Exploding Stars—an adventure that simulated a voyage through bursting white-hot supernovas. She saw the tall, twisting spires above the alien theaters and interplanetary opera houses. And in the center of the attractions Leia noticed the shining administration building, reflecting all the surrounding action like a gigantic mirror.

Upon making their arrival at the docking station, the *Falcon* landed.

"Princess, what do you say we take our honeymoon at Enchanted Lagoon?" Han asked. "They have a hologram flower grotto with flowers from every planet east of Endor and west of Tatooine."

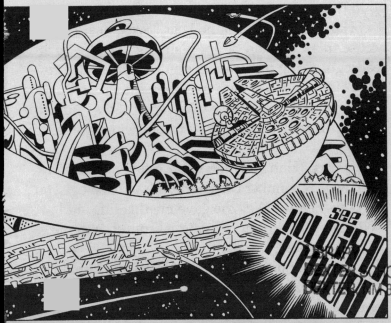

"Sounds like I'd probably start sneezing with all that pollen," Leia replied.

"No, the flowers at Enchanted Lagoon are just holograms—three-dimensional, totally lifelike images of flowers from other worlds. You can sniff them and touch them, but it's all just an illusion for the senses. There isn't a real flower growing within twelve million miles of this theme park."

As Leia and Han and the droids hurried down the *Falcon*'s exit ramp, incredible sights and sounds bombarded their eyes and ears: the dazzling fireworks high above at the top of the yellow dome, and thrilling music that boomed from 1,138 THX Ultrasound Speakers.

"If we're really going to make this official," Leia said, "we'd better buy rings for one another before we go to the altar."

Han put his arm around Leia. "Sweetheart, never accuse this Corellian of not planning ahead. I've already got a ring for you that you're going to adore."

"Han, you continue to surprise me. I thought your proposal of marriage was a spur of the moment thing. You know, I thought you were being spontaneous."

"I was," Han said, nervously biting his lower lip. "But, well, remember Dustangle, the archaeologist on the planet Duro? Well, he gave me this ring, and . . . well, I've been sort of carrying it around with me."

Leia smiled.

They dropped the two droids off at a Droid Repair Shop, leaving them for dent bodywork, scratch removal, and circuit adjustment. Han and Leia's next

stop was the shopping mall near the Asteroid Theater, with its marquee announcing a spectacular magic performance by Bithabus the Mystifier. To Leia's disappointment, the sign read: SOLD OUT FOR SIX MONTHS.

Leia led Han to a gem and jewelry store, where she began the overwhelming process of choosing Han's wedding ring. Han tried not to look. He stood with his back to the counter, studying a map of Hologram Fun World that was hanging on the wall.

"Princess, look at this!" Han exclaimed. "I can't believe it. I guess it's official—Lando's back in business!" He pointed to a portrait of their friend. Beneath the picture it read: LANDO CALRISSIAN, BARON ADMINISTRATOR OF HOLOGRAM FUN WORLD.

"Lando certainly bounced back quickly after losing his Cloud City governorship to Zorba the Hutt."

Han went to contact Lando on the comlink communication device. Meanwhile, Leia continued to look over the wedding bands. One ring in particular seemed to leap out of the display case and dazzle Leia's eyes. It was a gold band with four evenly spaced gems: a ruby, a sapphire, an emerald, and an amethyst. Leia spent all of her spare credits to buy Han the ring. To Leia's dismay, Han returned just as the salesman took the ring out of the display case and was about to put it into a small jewelry box.

"Good choice, Princess," Han said, getting a glimpse of the ring and its four colorful stones. "It's a beauty."

"Han, you sneak!" Leia said. "I didn't want you to see it until I gave it to you!"

"Sorry," Han replied. "I didn't know I'd be able

to reach Lando on the comlink so quickly."

Han and Leia left the gem and jewelry store and went to check up on Artoo-Detoo and See-Threepio, who were still waiting in line. It was the busiest Droid Repair Shop they had ever seen, which was just fine with Han.

Han went over to talk to the manager. "Do me a favor, okay?" Han asked, slipping the man a large tip. "Keep these droids real busy until later. Threepio has several dents and Artoo has circuit damage. And after they're fixed, give them both a double polish, a lubrication bath, and a memory upgrade." Han dropped his voice to a whisper. "My date and I would like to have a romantic night on the town—just the two of us, if you get what I mean."

"Happy to oblige you, Mr. Solo," the manager replied.

Lando Calrissian was concluding a meeting with the audit droids of Hologram Fun World when Han and Leia arrived in his reception room.

Grinning from ear to ear after hearing lots of good news about Fun World's profits, Lando hugged Leia as he stepped out of his office.

"What a treat!" Lando exclaimed. "Nothing could make me happier than to see that you're safe and sound, Princess." Lando kissed her on the cheek. "I nearly panicked when I had to surrender my job as Governor of Cloud City to that slime-ridden beast, Zorba the Hutt. I was afraid of what Zorba would do to you if he ever found you."

"We're no longer worried about Zorba," Han said reassuringly. "We tricked that slug into thinking that Leia is dead. Zorba thinks he destroyed the Princess when he blew up the Imperial Factory Barge back on Bespin."

Lando poured glasses of zoochberry juice for Leia, Han, and himself. "So what brings you to Hologram Fun World?" he asked. "Business or pleasure?"

"We're eloping," Han replied, gulping down his juice in one long swig. "My days as the galaxy's most carefree bachelor are about to come to an end."

Lando laughed. "Do my ears deceive me?" he asked. "So you finally popped the question to Leia, Han."

"He asked me and I said yes, and so here we are," Leia said with a smile.

"Well, I'm sorry I didn't ask you first, but be that as it may, this calls for a celebration!" Lando exclaimed with a wink. "Allow me to give you a little tour of our humble theme park."

In their time together, Han and Leia had zoomed through asteroid fields, fought against Death Stars side by side, battled Imperial stormtroopers, and warred against four-legged AT-AT walkers on planet Hoth. It was hard to believe, after all those experiences, that anything else could be even remotely more breathtaking.

But for the first time in their lives, thanks to the "total hologram experience" of Hologram Fun World, Han and Leia were overwhelmed. They went hoverskiing inside the mouth of an erupting volcano. Then they were swallowed by a huge Whaladon and swam their way out of its belly. They rode on the back of a star dragon as it leapt from a mountaintop and flew through the air. And they even drove a convertible cloud car right through the center of an exploding star!

To top off their visit, Leia made one of her fondest dreams come true. She took Han on a hologram fantasy voyage to Alderaan, her home planet, so Han could experience what it was like there before it was destroyed by Darth Vader and the Galactic Empire.

As they wandered arm in arm on a romantic walk down the picturesque side streets of Alderaan's largest city, Leia's mind activated Fun World's holographic projectors, so Han could see a world that now existed only in Leia's memories.

Then it all vanished as the ride to Alderaan came to an abrupt end. Once again they were back in the theme park.

"Well, if you two are still planning on getting married tonight," Lando said, "I'd say we have some work to do in order to get you both ready for your big moment."

Lando took them to a specialty boutique where one could buy or rent almost everything necessary for a wedding. The store had real bouquets, and Han selected a bouquet of purple roses from the moon of Endor. He handed the flowers to Princess Leia.

"I guess I was wrong about there not being any real flowers within twelve million miles of Fun World," Han admitted.

Then Han tried on several tuxedos until he found one that fit. Leia selected a very modern, white wedding dress with a long bridal veil.

"Pretty as a picture," Lando said. "And speaking of pictures, I've arranged for a droid photographer to do your wedding album. I want you to meet SB-9."

SB-9, short for Shutter-Bug-9, had a camera built into his chest. His eyes were strobe lights that flashed whenever he snapped a picture.

"Well, I guess the only thing left to do now is to take you to the thirteenth story of the administration building," Lando said, "so the Fun World Document Droids can check over your papers."

"What papers?" Han asked.

"Your I.D., of course," Lando explained.

"I.D.? What I.D.?" Han queried, sounding bewildered.

"You two have got your birth certificates with you, don't you?" Lando asked.

Han gulped. "Are you kidding? Mine's at my sky house back on Bespin."

"And my birth certificate was destroyed when the Empire blew up Alderaan," Leia explained. "Do you mean to tell me that we can't elope here unless we have our birth certificates with us?"

"Now, now—don't jump to any conclusions, Princess," Lando said reassuringly. "There's got to be an easy way around this problem. I'll see if the Document Bureau can print you up some new birth certificates right away. Simple as zoochberry pie. Except—"

Lando glanced at his watch, frowned, and rubbed his chin. "Uh-oh. The Document Bureau is already closed. We'll have to get your duplicate birth certificates tomorrow, first thing in the morning."

"But Leia and I were planning on getting married tonight," Han protested.

"Sorry," Lando said. "Bureaucracy. Normally I

could pull some strings and solve a little problem like this in a flash. But it's Fun World Founder's Day. Government offices here shut their doors early today. Everyone's gone home."

Noticing Leia's expression of disappointment, Lando added, "But don't despair. You'll get hitched by noon tomorrow, I guarantee it. In the meantime I have big plans for you two tonight. *Big plans,*" he repeated, winking with a mischievous smile.

CHAPTER 5
The Disappearance

As soon as the *Zorba Express* landed at Hologram Fun World, Zorba the Hutt called a meeting of the rogues and scoundrels who had come to work with him on the voyage. The purpose of the meeting was to plan the sabotage, theft, vandalism, and terrorism that Zorba hoped would ruin Fun World's appeal for tourists.

Meanwhile, Lando Calrissian was busy using his influence as Baron Administrator to get Han and Leia box-seat tickets for the next performance of Bithabus the Mystifier at the Asteroid Theater.

No sooner had the three of them entered the theater than trouble started a few blocks away. Zorba's gang of thieving bounty hunters set off a bomb blast at the Starlight Bank and made off with all the valuables from the safe-deposit boxes.

Elsewhere, outlaw alien bounty hunters were etching graffiti on the Hologram Fun World Administration Building with their laser pistols. And another group of thugs, led by Tibor the Barabel, barged into the Wonderbilt, one of the park's finest hotels, and robbed the guests of all their jewelry.

However, inside the Asteroid Theater, it was business as usual. The curtain lifted, and the best-known magic act in the galaxy began. Bithabus, a highly evolved Bith humanoid with a large head and large lidless black eyes, came out onstage to thunderous applause. Then Bithabus doubled in size before everyone's eyes, twisted himself like a pretzel, rolled across the stage floor, and magically turned into a droid very much like See-Threepio. The show was great fun, and Han, Leia, and Lando were having the time of their lives.

"A-haw-haw-haw . . . !" Zorba laughed, as the bounty hunters brought before him all the valuables they had just stolen.

Tibor placed some priceless earrings, bracelets, and necklaces into Zorba's hands. "Zorba," Tibor said, "this is no time for laughter. You've been tricked! You thought Princess Leia was dead. But Zorba—by the ghost of your great ancestor Kossak the Hutt, I swear Leia is still alive. And she's here in Fun World

right now!"

"Impossible!" Zorba raged. "She was trapped in the Imperial Factory Barge when we blew it up and sent it crashing into the Rethin Sea back on Bespin! No one could have escaped that explosion alive!"

"She must have gotten off the factory barge somehow before you destroyed it, Zorba. With my own eyes, I saw her enter the Asteroid Theater with Han Solo and Lando Calrissian! They're there watching the magic show of Bithabus the Mystifier!"

Zorba fumed, slurping his tongue in thought. "Princess Leia . . . alive? No!" Then he smacked his left fist into his right palm and grunted, "There will be no more mistakes. This time I'll watch with my own eyes as the princess takes her last breath—just like she watched my poor son Jabba choke to death. She'll die—right where Jabba did, on Tatooine at the Great Pit of Carkoon!"

Zorba's yellow reptilian eyes scanned the group of bounty hunters gathered before him. One of them was an alien of the same species as Bithabus. "You there—Cobak," Zorba said with a sneer. "You should be able to pass for Bithabus the Mystifier. I hope you can learn a little magic—fast!"

As the curtain rose after the intermission, Han, Leia, and Lando watched the performer come to the center of the stage. Bithabus silently looked out at the audience as though searching for someone. Han noticed that the magician's eyes seemed to meet Leia's glance.

"For my next trick," the magician said, "I'll need

a volunteer. I prefer a human. A lady, if possible."

The magician's eyes locked on Princess Leia. "You there, Miss!" he exclaimed. "Perhaps you would be kind enough to serve as my volunteer?"

"I was afraid of this," Leia whispered to Han. "Did I ever tell you about my stage fright?"

"Go on," Lando said. "You can't say no, Leia, it's for the good of the show! You'll have fun; come on."

Leia reluctantly got out of her box seat and went up to the stage.

"What planet are you from, Miss?" the Mystifier asked.

"The planet Bespin," Leia said, giving a phony reply. "I grew up in Cloud City."

"And your name?"

"Uhm—Zelda," Leia said. "Zelda Gizler."

"Married or single, Zelda?"

"Almost married," Leia said, smiling. "The big day is tomorrow."

"And what will your married name be, Zelda?" he asked.

"Kluggerhorn. Mrs. Zack Kluggerhorn."

Leia glanced at Han, who sat grimacing. She could see his lips shaping the words "Zack Kluggerhorn?" And then he pinched his nose in mock disgust.

"Well, congratulations, Zelda. If Mr. Kluggerhorn is here tonight, I'd like to assure him that all I'm going to do is shrink you down to the size of a pea—then we'll remove the space between your atoms so you'll be no bigger than a virus. Sound like fun? Of course it does. Come, just step inside this beautiful golden cage . . ."

Leia hesitated.

"You look upset, Zelda," the magician said. "There's absolutely nothing to fear. I can assure you, I'm not planning to ship you off to be a slave in the spice mines of Kessel!"

The audience broke out laughing. And so did the magician.

Everyone was having a wonderful time except Leia, who disliked the idea of having to climb inside the golden cage.

But all eyes in the theater were staring at her. Reluctantly Leia took a deep breath, told herself it was all in fun, and stepped inside the cage. The magician then slammed the door shut and locked it.

Suddenly two bounty hunters leapt out from behind the curtains at the wings of the stage.

TZZZZZT!!

The bounty hunters fired blasters at the power unit that controlled the lights.

TZZZZZZ . . . TZT . . . TZKLE . . .

The theater fell into total darkness, as the overhead illumination went out. Shrieks of fear came from the audience.

Then came blinding flashes of laserfire as more bounty hunters jumped out from their hiding places and fired randomly, creating panic in the theater.

Moments later, when the emergency lights came on, Han Solo was standing with his laserblaster in his hand, ready to fire. But the bounty hunters were gone. And so was the magician—*and* the golden cage

with Princess Leia!

Members of the Fun World Security Squad streamed into the theater, trying to calm the panicking audience.

Han and Lando jumped up onto the stage and glanced in all directions. There was no sign of Leia anywhere. Not even a single clue.

The *Zorba Express* blasted off and departed from Hologram Fun World.

Zorba and Tibor the Barabel alien bounty hunter were aboard, along with an extra passenger—Princess Leia!

Tibor had delivered the Princess directly to Zorba, still trapped inside the golden cage.

"A-haw-haw-haw . . . !" Zorba laughed cruelly. "So, Princess Leia, at last we meet. Allow me to introduce myself. I am Zorba, Jabba the Hutt's father," he exclaimed. "And *nobody* is better at getting even with a murdering Princess like you than a clever old Hutt like me!"

"I never murdered anyone," Leia said defiantly. "I'm a diplomat. I believe one should settle disputes using peaceful negotiations—unless one is attacked and has to defend herself."

"And I suppose you were only defending yourself when you killed my son, Jabba," Zorba said in a mocking tone. "Tell me, Princess Leia, did you think Jabba's papa would allow his son's death to go unavenged? Did you really think you would get away with your crime?"

"Jabba is the one who committed crimes," Leia

insisted, clenching her fists in rising anger. "More crimes than I can count. He was a gangster and a smuggler and a thief. And you're as greedy, and just as wretched and monsterous as he was!"

"Tsk tsk tsk," Zorba said, waving his forefinger as a warning. "If you had longer to live, I would teach you some manners, Princess Leia. But what's the use of teaching manners to a human who will die in a few hours anyway? It's a waste of time and precious energy that could be used for better things. Like eating."

Zorba waved his forefinger in Leia's direction once again and continued to scold her. "I know that you murdered Jabba in his sail barge at the Great Pit of Carkoon on Tatooine. You twisted a chain around his neck—"

"It was the chain that held me prisoner!" Leia protested. "I was only trying to get free. That's every prisoner's right!"

"I've heard how you twisted that chain around poor Jabba, squeezing the breath out of my son. Prisoner's right, indeed. Well, he didn't get to see his prisoner die that day at the Great Pit of Carkoon. But I'll make up for it, Princess. I'm going to take you to Tatooine and drop you into the pit—right into the Mouth of Sarlacc!"

Zorba slurped and slobbered just thinking about it. "You know, Princess, it takes the Sarlacc a period of one thousand years to digest its victims," he continued. "So for a thousand years you'll be trapped there in its stomach, until there's nothing left of you— not even your bones! A-haw-haw-haw . . . !"

Leia wished she could reverse everything that had happened to her since Lando told her that her marriage to Han would have to wait until morning. If only she could have retraced her steps, and not gone to the theater. If only she hadn't gone up on the stage and climbed into the cage. . . .

"You're not my only prisoner aboard this ship," Zorba said with a leering grin. "There's an old friend of yours here too. Perhaps you'd like to say hello!"

Zorba pushed a lever on his control panel, causing a door in the wall behind Leia's golden cage to slide open. Leia's pulse quickened as she glanced inside.

There she saw a solid block of black carbonite! And sticking partially out of the block, frozen alive in suspended animation, was the three-eyed Imperial tyrant who until recently had been the evil ruler of the Empire—

"—Trioculus!" Leia gasped.

CHAPTER 6
The Mofference

Exploring the storage area beneath the stage of the Asteroid Theater, Han and Lando discovered Bithabus the Mystifier tied up inside a bright red cabinet that was a spare prop for the magic show.

FWAAAAP!

A short, well-aimed blast from Han's laserblaster burned through the ropes that were fastened to the magician's wrists and legs.

"What happened? How'd you get locked inside that cabinet, Bithabus?" Han asked.

"It all happened so fast I can hardly remember," Bithabus replied. "During the intermission, I can recall being suddenly surrounded by bounty hunters. Then they ordered me to take off my costume. There was another Bith with them—they called him Cobak. He seemed to be one of their gang. Cobak put on my costume and said something about taking my place on stage for the second act." Bithabus got up and dusted himself off. "I think I recall someone saying this was Zorba the Hutt's trap to catch Princess Leia," he added.

"That slimy, foul, disgusting, ugly, odorous, slobbering, dirty rotten slug!" Han exclaimed, pounding his fist against the wall in anger.

"There was a reptilian bounty hunter with sharp teeth talking about the plan," Bithabus continued. "They called him Tibor. He told Cobak that Zorba was going to settle his score with the princess once and for all."

"Naturally," Lando said. "Getting even with their enemies is all Hutts know how to do. If it wasn't for their thrill in taking revenge, every Hutt in the galaxy would probably roll over and die of boredom."

"I can remember Tibor's words," Bithabus added. "He said, 'Leia's punishment will fit her crime!'"

"Aha!" Han said, snapping his fingers. "Lucky for us that I know how that slobbering slug thinks. Leia strangled Jabba the Hutt at the Pit of Carkoon. So Zorba is probably taking Leia to the planet Tatooine—straight to the pit!"

Lando sighed in dismay. "I hoped I'd never see that disgusting place again, but I guess that just wasn't my destiny."

"Thanks, old buddy, for helping me out," Han said, slapping his friend on the back.

"I wouldn't miss a chance to give Zorba a taste of his own slimy medicine," Lando replied.

Han and Lando said good-bye to Bithabus, then bolted up the ladder to the stage floor and ran out of the Asteroid Theater. Once outside they turned in the direction of the *Millennium Falcon*'s docking bay. "Just a second," Han said. "We're forgetting Threepio and Artoo!"

Han and Lando turned around and quickly dashed off to the Droid Repair Shop. They yanked Threepio and Artoo out of the building before the droids' polish was even dry. "*Tziiiiit gnig fzoooop!*" Artoo-Detoo protested. But as they proceeded back toward to the spaceship docking zone, Han quickly explained to the droids what had happened to Leia.

The four of them hurried up the entry ramp of the *Millennium Falcon* and into the navigation room. "Well, I notice quite a few upgrades and custom modifications since I used to own this baby," Lando said, glancing around the space freighter. "You'd think I would have learned my lesson about gambling when I lost the *Millennium Falcon* to you in that bet we made." Lando strapped himself into the seat next to Han. "Does the ship still make a whining sound when you give it the juice?"

"No way," Han replied. "She purrs like a mooka now." Han reached for the controls, turning on the power thrusters. "We're going to haul it from here to Tatooine in thirty-three standard time parts, or my name is Zack Kluggerhorn."

"Are you losing your touch, Han?" a familiar sounding female voice said from behind Han's shoulder. "I should think you could make it there in thirty time parts or less."

Han and Lando turned in shock. Who else was inside the spaceship?

"Leia!" they both exclaimed.

"Why are you planning on departing for Tatooine?" Leia asked. "And especially in such a rush?"

Suddenly Han noticed something different about the princess's eyes and became suspicious. "Wait a minute," he said, "you're not Leia!"

"Of course I am," she replied.

"Then what are the four colors of the stones on the wedding ring you bought for me?" he challenged.

"Why should I tell you and spoil the surprise?" she asked.

"Aha!" Han exclaimed. "The real Leia would know it's not a surprise, because I already saw the ring when we were in the jewelry store. You're the Project Decoy Human Replica Droid."

Suddenly Luke Skywalker popped out from behind the large, horizontal stabilizer at the rear of the cockpit. "I never could fool you, Han," Luke said.

Ken poked his head out too, smiling with delight at being able to surprise Han and Lando. "Fugo fixed the laser unit in the droid's eyes, Han," Ken said.

Luke explained. "When Mon Mothma received an emergency intelligence report that both the *Millennium Falcon* and the *Zorba Express* were heading for

Hologram Fun World," Luke said, "we figured we'd better check up on you two. Chewie wanted to come, too, but Mon Mothma decided he should stay behind in case they needed help keeping Triclops under control."

"So you're here to spy on me and Leia," Han said, frowning in disgust. "Can't a guy even sneak away on personal business once in a while without everybody in the Alliance finding out about it?"

"Your business on this trip is no longer personal, Han," Luke continued. "You proposed marriage to my sister—the gossip's all over Fun World. Welcome to the family!"

"Save the congratulations until we get the bride back safely," Han replied. "Leia's in deep, deep—"

Han's words, as he continued to fill the others in, were drowned out by the sound of the spaceship's engines roaring to life. The *Millennium Falcon* accelerated as fast as its sublight-speed thrusters would permit it to go—and then it made the hyperspace jump and exceeded light speed.

Neither the passengers aboard the *Millennium Falcon* nor those on the *Zorba Express* had any way of knowing that at that very moment a large Imperial spaceship was orbiting the planet Tatooine. It was the Moffship, the official space vehicle of the Imperial grand moffs—the Imperial governors of the outer regions of space.

The grand moffs were holding a secret conference—a Mofference. And leading the secret Mofference was razor-toothed Grand Moff Hissa, whose body had been nearly destroyed by a torrential flood of liquid toxic waste back on the planet Duro.

Grand Moff Hissa would never forget how High Prophet Jedgar had left him to die in the underground caverns of Duro. A stormtrooper saved Hissa's life, lifting him out of the bubbling acid slime that had eaten through his body. If the Prophets of the Dark Side were allowed to have their way, Grand Moff Hissa would not have lived to tell the tale; as it was, Hissa survived, although he lost both his arms and his legs.

Grand Moff Hissa adjusted his mechanical hoverchair to raise it a few inches above the floor as he presided over the Mofference.

Hissa was outfitted with mechanical arms, which had been taken from an Imperial droid and surgically attached to his shoulders. The liquid toxic waste had eaten away his body all the way up to his hip bone, leaving no stump for attaching any mechanical legs. The feisty and embittered grand moff would now have to spend the rest of his life confined to a hoverchair.

"Any Prophet of the Dark Side who approaches and tries to enter our Moffship will be taken hostage," Hissa declared. "That's our only way to bargain with Kadann, and save what little power we grand moffs have left in the Empire, now that Kadann has declared himself to be the new Imperial leader!"

Grand Moff Dunhausen toyed with his earrings that were shaped like little laserblasters. "I heard a rumor from a high-ranking Imperial intelligence agent that Kadann wants to disband the grand moffs com-

pletely!" he said, snarling.

"I heard the same rumor," Grand Moff Muzzer added, puffing his fat cheeks in and out nervously. "Kadann wants to take each one of us aside and demote us. It is rumored he'll strip us of our power and appoint us to low-ranking military positions on the most slime-ridden and frozen planets in the galaxy."

"Kadann hates us because we were loyal to Trioculus to the very end," Grand Moff Thistleborn said. "But with Trioculus as Emperor, at least we had influence and shared the rule of the Empire."

Suddenly Emdee-Five, the Imperial droid, knocked on the thick metal door of the spaceship's large, secluded Mofference room. "Excuse my intrusion," Emdee said, "however, I thought you should all be aware that a Huttian spacecraft has been spied approaching Tatooine, due north of our position. It appears to be the *Zorba Express*."

"Zorba the Hutt!" Grand Moff Hissa exclaimed, gnashing together his spiked, razor-sharp teeth.

"Zorba's the wretched beast who captured Trioculus, froze our leader in carbonite, and then hung him up in the Cloud City Museum!" Grand Moff Muzzer declared.

"Curse the day that Kadann vaporized Trioculus with neutron beams," Grand Moff Dunhausen fumed. "If it weren't for Zorba the Hutt, it never would have happened!"

At the rear of the Moffship was a tractor beam projector—perfect for enabling a large spaceship to swallow a smaller one.

And so, at Hissa's orders, the grand moffs aimed

their powerful tractor beam at the *Zorba Express*, drawing it closer . . . and closer . . .

Meanwhile, Han's spaceship had just come out of hyperdrive and was decelerating as it approached the desert world of Tatooine. A safe distance away, Han Solo, Luke Skywalker, Ken, Lando Calrissian, and the droids were witnessing the scene between the Moffship and the *Zorba Express* play out from inside the *Millennium Falcon*.

"Looks like our luck has run out," Han said, shaking his head in dismay. "Now we not only have to rescue Princess Leia from Zorba the Hutt, but from the grand moffs as well!"

CHAPTER 7
Trioculus Restored

The grand moffs surrounded the *Zorba Express*, which was now inside a heavily armored chamber within the Moffship.

"Stormtroopers, break open the boarding hatch!" Hissa shouted from his hover-chair.

But the boarding hatch of the *Zorba Express* popped open before the stormtroopers had to apply force. Facing the stormtroopers and the grand moffs was Tibor the bounty hunter, armed with a laserblaster in each hand. Tibor took aim at every grand moff he could see, while Zorba stood behind him, raising a portable laser cannon.

"Take them alive!" Hissa screamed, as he retreated. Hissa used his mechanized hover-chair to dodge the laserfire flying around the chamber. But not all the grand moffs were able to successfully avoid being targets. One of Tibor's blasts struck Grand Moff Muzzer in the right leg.

Stormtrooper reinforcements came pouring in from every direction, armed with force pikes—long poles topped with power tips used to stun an enemy.

As the stormtroopers began to gain the advantage, Grand Moff Hissa maneuvered his hover-chair to the nearby supply cabinet. He reached for a projectile launcher with a fully armed four-cannister magazine. Aiming directly at the cockpit of the *Zorba Express*, Hissa began firing a round of projectiles that contained smoke, gas, and chemical agents.

The cockpit quickly filled with lung irritants. As Zorba and Tibor began coughing and choking, they were overpowered by charging stormtroopers who jabbed them with the force pikes. Tibor tumbled to the floor of the chamber, unconscious. He was quickly taken away to the prisoner bay area near the flight crew stations.

Zorba's stubby hands were chained together as his coughing fit continued. His yellow, reptilian eyes were unable to shed tears, but they became red, glassy, and moist.

The stormtroopers forced Zorba to squirm his huge body down a ramp, prodded every wiggle of the way by force pikes.

Grand Moff Thistleborn attached the chain connecting Zorba's wrists to a hoist, while Grand Moff Muzzer, despite his wounded leg, managed to walk over to the lever used to raise the hoist high above the floor.

"You grand moffs think you can break old Zorba!" the Hutt shouted. The chain then pulled his sluglike body up into the air by his wrists and let him dangle. "Curse you all! A-haw-haw-haw . . . !"

Grand Moff Hissa maneuvered his hover-chair over to the *Zorba Express*. He set his chair down inside and glanced around. An irritating smell burned his nostrils. It wasn't the coughing gas from the projectile launcher—it was the smell of frozen carbonite.

"I want every inch of the *Zorba Express* searched—

from its Telgorn flight computers to its rear bulk storage compartments!" Hissa shouted.

Several stormtroopers ran immediately up the ramp and entered the *Zorba Express*. They began their search at the front of the navigation room.

Soon they located a storage door that was suspiciously disguised as part of the hull of the ship. Hissa's strong metal hands pushed away the power coupler that was hiding the door's latch. Inhaling sharply and then holding his breath, he pried with all his strength and pulled the door open.

Behind the door, encased in frozen carbonite, was Trioculus. Hissa gasped.

"Our Dark Lord!" Hissa exclaimed, his eyes bulging in disbelief. A series of images rushed through Hissa's mind all at once—Trioculus as Supreme Slavelord of Kessel working thousands of slaves to death in the spice mines . . . Trioculus trying to electrocute Luke Skywalker inside the Whaladon hunting submarine . . . Trioculus scheming to bomb the Rebel Alliance Senate . . . and Trioculus burning the rain forests of Yavin as he searched for the Jedi Prince, Ken, whom he was determined to destroy at any cost.

"But . . . how is it possible that Trioculus still exists?" Grand Moff Hissa wondered. "Kadann destroyed the carbonite block with fiery neutron beams."

From outside the *Zorba Express*, Hissa could hear the Hutt's laughter. "A-haw-haw-haw . . . !" Zorba taunted the grand moffs. "Did you really think I'd be stupid enough to put the *real* carbonite block that contained Trioculus on display in the Cloud City Museum? Kadann destroyed nothing but a statue of your so-called 'Dark Lord.' I tricked him good—tricked you all!"

"You continue searching the ship!" Grand Moff Hissa ordered several stormtroopers. To another group of stormtroopers he snapped, "Remove this block of carbonite and take it to the power modulator. Then send a low-level current from the modulator to the carbonite and melt it, setting Trioculus free!"

The heavy carbonite block was carried from the *Zorba Express* and melted at once, thawing Trioculus from his state of suspended animation. Slowly Trioculus emerged from the carbonization in which he had been frozen, a mindless state in which his lifeless body remained more dead than alive.

The three-eyed tyrant took one breath, then another, grimacing and gritting his teeth as though each inhalation wracked him with pain. As Hissa remained at his side, Trioculus's breaths slowly began to flow more naturally, and the agony of his first moments of release from the carbonite faded.

Trioculus blinked and cleared his three eyes of the last bits of carbonite. "Hisssssa?" he gasped, as he slowly regained his sight.

"Yes, my Dark Lordship. It is I!"

"What's happened to you, Hissa?"

"I lost my arms and legs in what you might call an industrial accident, your Lordship," the grand moff explained. "But don't fret about me. All that matters now is that you're alive—and that you can bring Kadann under control again and lead the Empire to new dark and glorious victories against the Rebel Alliance!"

"What has Kadann done?" Trioculus asked. "He's remained loyal to me, has he not? He gave me his dark blessing and accepted me as ruler of the Empire."

"That is correct, Trioculus," Grand Moff Hissa replied. "But while you were frozen in carbonite, Kadann took back his dark blessing and declared himself to be the new Imperial ruler."

"Curse him, then," Trioculus declared, "and may the cosmic radiation of the Null Zone bake his brain."

"The Prophets of the Dark Side can no longer be trusted," Hissa continued. "A prophet named Jedgar left me for dead in a puddle of toxic slime."

Leading the way in his hover-chair, Grand Moff Hissa took Trioculus on a tour of the Moffship. As they proceeded through a corridor filled with weapons systems, Trioculus recounted the times he had employed the different weapons to slaughter helpless humans and aliens—the antiorbital ion cannon that had blasted many tourist spaceships that had accidently strayed into Imperial restricted zones . . . the turbolaser that had mowed down thousands of protesting slaves during the slave rebellion on Kessel . . . the C-136 "Grandfather Gun" Trioculus had used to blow up a dam and flood troublesome settlers in the Grand Kessel River Valley . . .

As Trioculus recounted his merciless murders of days gone by, the sound of laughter and taunts echoed throughout the Moffship.

"That's Zorba the Hutt carrying on like a fool," Grand Moff Hissa explained. "Perhaps you can make him understand that his situation is no laughing matter. We grand moffs have tried, but he only laughs more."

Grand Moff Hissa took Trioculus through the Moffship, until they were face-to-face with Zorba the Hutt, who was still hanging by his wrists.

"Zorba!" Trioculus exclaimed, staring into the reddened eyes of his old enemy. "You'll regret the day you decided to freeze me in carbonite! I should chop your carcass up into little pieces and feed you to hungry Fefze beetles!"

"If you do that," Zorba said, "then you'll never see Princess Leia alive again."

"What do you know about Princess Leia?" Trioculus demanded.

"I'm the only one in the galaxy who knows where she is," Zorba replied. "I was planning to execute her at the Great Pit of Carkoon on Tatooine. But seeing as how you're such a dear old friend, if you free me from these chains and spare my life, I might decide to tell you where she is and let you have her."

The very mention of Princess Leia's name quickened Trioculus's breath. Trioculus longed to make Leia appreciate the ways of darkness and evil. And when the princess understood and respected the power of the Dark Side, then Trioculus would take her as his bride!

"Let the Hutt down at once," Trioculus declared.

"But my Dark Lordship—" Grand Moff Muzzer protested.

"At once, I said," Trioculus thundered.

Grand Moff Muzzer lowered the hoist, and Zorba's body settled down solidly on the floor.

"Unchain his hands!" Trioculus demanded.

The order was quickly obeyed.

"Now then, Zorba," Trioculus said with a slight glimmer of a smile. "I've kept up my end of our bargain. You're unchained. Now tell me where I can find Princess Leia—or you'll still end up as a snack for Fefze beetles after all!"

"Patience," Zorba said. "You don't have to look very far. Princess Leia is much closer than you would dare hope."

At that, Zorba squirmed up the ramp to his spaceship. Trioculus followed right behind him.

"This way," Zorba declared. "If your stormtroopers had been clever enough, they would have found her already."

Zorba opened the door to the cargo bay. Trioculus's evil heart skipped a beat as his eyes beheld the golden cage—with Princess Leia trapped inside.

The cage was moved at once to Grand Moff Hissa's private quarters aboard the Moffship. Trioculus remained by her side, alone with the woman he loved.

Leia gave Trioculus the silent treatment, as the three-eyed slavelord sat beside her cage, reminding the princess how well she had been treated the last time he had captured her—back on the Imperial Factory Barge on the planet Bespin.

"The most powerful man in the galaxy, Master of the Dark Side and ruler of the Galactic Empire, commands that you accept his fond affection," Trioculus addressed her. "Will you renounce the Rebel Alliance and give me your hand in marriage, Princess Leia?"

"Sorry to spoil your demented plans, Trioculus," Princess Leia replied with a sneer. "But I've already accepted a marriage proposal from Han Solo."

"Han Solo!" Trioculus repeated with a grimace. "The Rebel Corellian cargo pilot? Do you think for one moment that he can offer you what *I* can? Will he grant you starships to command? Planets to rule?"

"Kadann seems to think that *he* rules the Empire, Trioculus," Leia snapped. "The Prophets of the Dark Side say you're a has-been. Word is out that you're nothing but a fake and a fraud who lied about being the son of Emperor Palpatine."

"My dispute with the Prophets of the Dark Side is none of your affair," Trioculus replied. "Your attitude, Princess, must really undergo a *drastic* change, if you ever hope to get out of that cage." The tyrant paused for a moment to think. "How would you enjoy watching Zorba the Hutt tossed into the Mouth of Sarlacc? Would it thrill you?"

"Do with Zorba as you like," Leia said.

"I gave my word to Zorba that I would free him," Trioculus declared. "But if you would like him dead, Leia, I would gladly make him suffer the fate he planned for you. Wouldn't the thrill of revenge delight you?"

"The Empire blew up my home planet of Alderaan," Leia replied, clutching the bars of her cage. "The Empire snuffs out freedom and liberty wherever it exists. They murder the brave soldiers of the Alliance, who fight to bring back the laws and justice of the Old Republic. If you're really the ruler of the Empire as you claim, Trioculus, then you're a thousand times more of an enemy to me than Zorba the Hutt."

"So, you still refuse to accept me, and you continue to scorn my affection and noble intentions toward you," Trioculus said, narrowing all three of his eyes.

"I scorn everything about you!" Leia replied. "Don't think I've forgotten that you burned the rain forests of Yavin Four, Trioculus—all because you wanted to find the entrance to the Lost City of the Jedi and destroy our Jedi Prince, a mere boy!"

"Perhaps you'd prefer that I turn you back over to Zorba then, my Princess," Trioculus said, letting his smile dissolve into a wicked sneer. "What would you have to say to that?"

But Leia said nothing.

"Your answer is yes, then? You choose to be with Zorba, rather than with me? Quickly—speak, or you shall seal your fate forever!"

Leia knew she had to buy time. Surely Han had

figured out what happened to her by now. But would SPIN send a rescue mission? Or would her own Jedi powers have to aid her somehow in finding a means to escape? Everything Leia had tried to do failed her so far—including the Jedi mind-clouding technique, which had no effect upon Trioculus at all.

"Don't give me over to Zorba," she said through clenched teeth.

"So," Trioculus said smoothly, clasping his hands together, "I'm making progress with you then. You prefer *my* charming company to the company of that slobbering slug, Zorba."

Trioculus departed, leaving Princess Leia in her golden cage. He then returned to the large chamber where stormtroopers stood guard over Zorba the Hutt.

Trioculus turned to Grand Moff Hissa. "Make preparations for my wedding, Hissa," he ordered. "Find the Dark Book of Imperial Justice, and I'll show you the passage that you're to read at the ceremony. We'll hold the wedding here in the Moffship, just as soon as we've sent Zorba the Hutt to his doom. He's to be swallowed by the Mouth of Sarlacc, as planned!"

"You gave me your word, Trioculus!" Zorba stormed.

"I only keep my word to those who have never betrayed me," Trioculus replied. "I'm surprised you didn't know that, Zorba. In the short time you have remaining, perhaps you'll come to regret that you froze me in carbonite." Trioculus turned to Grand Moff Dunhausen. "Tell the pilots at the command console to descend to Tatooine," he commanded. "Our destination is the Great Pit of Carkoon, beyond the

Dune Sea."

Zorba merely chortled. He then spit in Trioculus's direction, spraying the nearby stormtroopers with the saliva of a fearless old Hutt.

CHAPTER 8
The Imperial Wedding

In a scorched desert region on Tatooine, the Mouth of Sarlacc swallowed its latest meal—an elephantlike Bantha beast and a Tusken Raider.

Riding the Bantha, the sand creature had come foolishly close to the edge of the Great Pit of Carkoon to satisfy his curiosity. He had heard the legends of the huge and awesome mouth at the bottom of the pit—a mouth that devoured every living creature that had the misfortune to stumble into it.

But the Tusken Raider hadn't planned on his Bantha stepping on a prickly cacta bush—or that his

Bantha would leap to free himself from the thick thorns and tumble into the pit, headfirst.

While the Mouth of Sarlacc gobbled its noontime meal beneath the heat of Tatooine's blistering twin suns, the Moffship slowly descended from the sky.

No one on board the Moffship observed the *Millennium Falcon* as it approached. The *Falcon* flew within a narrow zone, staying in the ship's blind spot, undetected by the Novaldex deflector shield at the Moffship's rear. Then the *Falcon* attached itself to the ship's upper access hatch and rode piggyback.

Inside the Moffship, the crew was busy navigating above the Dune Sea, where heat waves from the desert sand caused strong winds. The grand moffs gathered at the armored viewport—a large, round window in the floor—to look for the Great Pit of Carkoon.

There was one Imperial who might have detected the *Millennium Falcon*—an intelligence specialist assigned to security duties at the stern of the Moffship. But he was too busy repairing damage caused by laserfire from the battle with Zorba and Tibor to notice the Alliance freighter.

Han, Luke, Ken, and Lando, accompanied by the Human Replica Droid of Leia, popped open the upper access hatch and crawled into the Moffship totally unnoticed.

"This is folly," See-Threepio said, waving his golden arms frantically and calling after the others in a loud whisper. "It's suicide. You'll never get out of the Moffship alive. And when the grand moffs find me and Artoo, they'll deactivate us for sure and use us as spare parts for their assassin droids!"

"Cool your circuits, Threepio," Han said over his shoulder. "The grand moffs will never catch you two droids, because you and Artoo are going to stay behind in the *Falcon* and wait for us. I want Artoo to fix the hum in the Carbanti 29L electromagnetic package. And while he's doing that, I want you to give a power boost to the hyperdrive multiplier so we'll be ready to get out of here in a hurry when we return."

"Artoo and I will never see any of you again, I just know it," See-Threepio complained, continuing his nervous chatter. "Oh, dear. And if you must know, I strongly disagree with your decision to take the Human Replica Droid with you. What if Fugo did something wrong when he tried to fix her? What if one of you gets a laserblast to the heart like Fandar did? It's unthinkable. Master Luke, won't *you* listen to reason?"

"You're overruled, Threepio," Luke responded. "We know what we're doing. Now listen to Han. You have work to do."

The five of them continued on as the Human Replica Droid led them into a ventilation shaft.

"You're sure you can find Leia?" Lando Calrissian whispered to the droid.

"Of course I'm sure," the Human Replica Droid replied. "It's one of my primary functions."

"I just hope Threepio doesn't turn out to be right this time," Han said. He then pulled himself up from the ventilation shaft two floors above the private chambers that were reserved for the grand moffs. "This could turn out to be like looking for a microchip lost in a field of zoochberries."

"Don't worry, Han, this is going to be simple," the Human Replica Droid explained. "When Fandar and Fugo designed me, they installed a homing mechanism so that I can find Leia anywhere. Even now, I can detect the vibrations of her biorhythm. We'll find her. Just keep your finger on the trigger of your blaster and follow me."

The Moffship was now hovering directly above the Great Pit of Carkoon. Looking through the armored viewport, Grand Moff Muzzer pointed out to Grand Moff Thistleborn the gigantic mouth in the sand below them.

Ten stormtroopers surrounded Zorba in the viewing area, keeping the Hutt under guard. They were dressed in sandtrooper uniforms, ready in case Trioculus required them to set foot on Tatooine. Each stormtrooper wore an eighteen-piece antiblaster cocoon shell with a heat-reflective coating, a helmet with breathing filters, and a utility belt that had a food-and-water pack.

Thrusting out his chest confidently and ceremoniously, Trioculus led Princess Leia to see Zorba. Once again the Hutt was hoisted up by his wrists, this time dangling in the air directly above the viewport window.

"Curse your parents and grandparents for ten generations!" Zorba hissed.

Trioculus ignored the Hutt. He pointed through the viewport in the floor. Zorba's yellow, reptilian eyes glanced down to see where the Imperial ruler was directing his attention.

"That's where you wanted to send Leia," Trioculus snapped. "But now it's you who shall be executed instead. Go to your death, Zorba—and die like the slug you are!"

Trioculus touched a red button on the wall. The viewport window in the floor began opening wide, like an immense porthole, as Trioculus did his best to imitate Zorba's famous laugh. "Ah-ha-ha-haaaa!"

Trioculus suddenly released the chain that was holding Zorba over the hole, letting the old Hutt plunge to the scorching sands of Tatooine down below. "Who's laughing now, Zorba?" Trioculus called after him.

Everyone on board the Moffship watched as the Hutt struck the ground just below the upper rim of the pit. Zorba rolled and tumbled downward, and the Mouth of Sarlacc opened wide to greet him.

The sound of the wind was too strong for anyone to hear well. However, standing near the viewport of the Moffship, Grand Moff Hissa thought he heard Zorba's screaming moan just as the tentaclelike tongue of the Sarlacc wrapped around Zorba, yanking the Hutt into its immense mouth.

The mouth sucked Zorba down past its sharp teeth and belched. Then it closed, trapping Zorba inside its stomach. There, acids would digest the old Hutt for the next one thousand years.

All the while, Trioculus fixed his three eyes on Princess Leia, rather than on the Mouth of Sarlacc and Zorba. Trioculus saw Leia sigh with relief, perhaps even smile, as he had predicted. Or was it just a

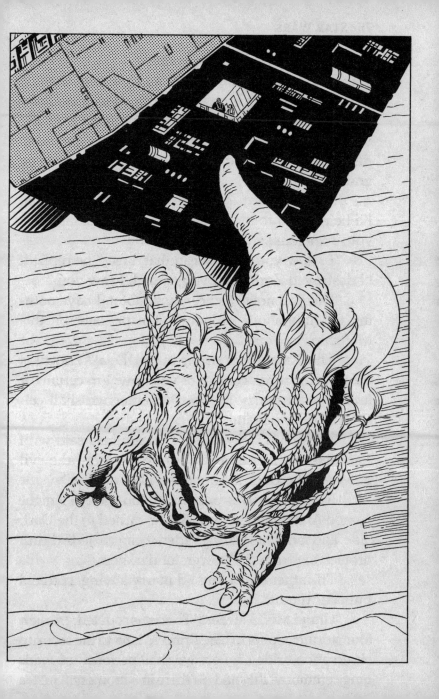

grimace? He couldn't be certain.

Then Leia closed her eyes and glanced away.

"This day has brought me three victories, Princess," Trioculus declared. "First, I was freed from the carbonite. Then Zorba paid for the injustice he did to me—and to you. And lastly, I have taught you to be grateful to me."

"Grateful to you?" Leia exclaimed. "Guess again. I'll be grateful to the Alliance when they assassinate you, Trioculus."

"I know you don't mean that, Leia," he replied. "I destroyed Zorba and you smiled. I saw you."

"Did you now? I sincerely doubt it. I have nothing to smile about as long as I'm prisoner on this Moffship."

"The Dark Side is strong in you, Leia!" Trioculus continued. "It has control of you now; I'm certain of it. You shall marry me, and together we shall celebrate Zorba's death!"

"Dream on, Trioculus," Princess Leia said with clenched teeth. "I'm a Jedi, protected from the evil power of the Dark Side and the likes of you."

"Your father was once a Jedi too—a Jedi Knight named Anakin Skywalker. But he turned to the Dark Side and became Darth Vader. Being a Jedi didn't protect *him* from the powers of darkness."

"I'd rather die before I'd marry a lying, ruthless Imperial tyrant."

"Grand Moff Muzzer!" Trioculus shouted. "Assign four stormtroopers to take Princess Leia to the security observation bridge, where we shall perform the wedding ceremony! I'll join you there in a moment."

* * *

Luke Skywalker, Han Solo, Ken, Lando Calrissian, and the Human Replica Droid of Leia were watching and listening to every word Trioculus said. They were crouched down in a sheltered corner of the chamber, hiding behind the large, thick gray frame that housed one of the Moffship's gyroscopic stabilizers.

As the four stormtroopers took Princess Leia down a corridor toward the security observation bridge, they brushed very close to where Luke and the others were hiding.

"Now," whispered Luke, signaling to his friends. With Luke in the lead, followed by Han, Ken, Lando, and then the Human Replica Droid, they took off down the corridor and silently overpowered the four stormtroopers.

"Han!" Princess Leia exclaimed, her eyes widening with excitement. And then she saw the others. "Luke! Lando, Ken! How did you ever find me? And what are you doing here?" she said to the Human Replica Droid.

"No time for a play-by-play description now, Princess," Han said, taking her in his arms. "You're safe, that's all that matters."

"Let's try on these stormtrooper uniforms for size," Luke said. There was no time to lose.

The stormtrooper uniforms fit Luke and Han with room to spare. It was a snug fit for Lando, but even the one that belonged to the shortest stormtrooper was several sizes too large for Ken.

"Tuck those pant legs deep into the boots, kid, and puff out your chest like this," Han said, trying to help Ken fill out the oversized uniform. "That'll have to do for now . . ."

They then picked up the four unconscious stormtroopers one at a time and dropped them off in the nearest garbage chute.

"Proceed to the security observation bridge," Luke said to the Human Replica Droid. "You know what to do." The droid shook her head and wished them luck. She then took off down the corridor.

Han turned to Princess Leia and took her by the arm. "Princess, make like a prisoner. We've got a date aboard the *Millennium Falcon*, at the upper entry portal. Let's get out of here!"

Their helmets securely in place, Luke took hold of Leia's other arm. Together they marched in step, with Lando and Ken following along from behind.

"Do you think the Human Replica Droid will make it to Trioculus's wedding ceremony?" Han asked. "The Imperials are going to wonder where her guards are."

"She'll make it," Luke said, "even if she has to dispose of every last Imperial who stands in her way."

Trioculus entered the security observation bridge with Grand Moff Hissa floating in his hover-chair at his side. Glancing around, Trioculus noticed that the stormtroopers who were supposed to be guarding Leia weren't there. But the Human Replica Droid, whom he mistook for Leia herself, was standing there awaiting him. She appeared to be in a cooperative mood, even though no guards were present.

"You look lovely, my dear," the Imperial tyrant said, thrusting out his chest in military fashion. "And the moment you've secretly dreamed of for so long has now arrived. Princess Leia, you're about to become my bride!" Then he drew his right hand from behind his back, revealing a dozen black zinthorn flowers. "For you," he said. "A wedding bouquet."

Without resisting, Leia accepted the horrible zinthorns. Then Grand Moff Hissa, who was to perform the wedding ceremony, steered his hover-chair behind the turbolaser access shaft, which stuck up from the floor and looked vaguely like a wedding altar.

One by one the other grand moffs filed into the security observation bridge to witness the ceremony.

"I hope Trioculus isn't making a mistake," Grand Moff Muzzer whispered to Grand Moff Thistleborn. "It's a bit too soon to know for sure whether Leia has embraced the Dark Side."

"He knows exactly what he's doing," Thistleborn replied with a nod. "Consider how loyal Darth Vader was to Emperor Palpatine and the Dark Side. We must never forget that the Princess is Vader's daughter—his flesh and blood."

"Yes, but so is Luke Skywalker," Grand Moff Muzzer replied softly. "And a more nettlesome troublemaker than Skywalker we'll never find."

Grand Moff Hissa opened the Dark Book of Imperial Justice and began reading aloud. "We are witnesses to a momentous event," he began, "the marriage of our Imperial ruler to Princess Leia Organa, who shall now of her own free will re-

nounce the Rebel Alliance and offer her eternal allegiance to the Dark Side! Thus, Leia will prepare herself to follow in the path of her father, Darth Vader, and at last shall become our queen—the Queen of the Empire!

"But first, some fitting words for this occasion," Hissa continued. He cleared his throat and began reading: "By Imperial law, when the Emperor takes a wife, she becomes his property, obliged to obey his every word and bow down before him whenever he wishes a show of obedience."

The corners of Trioculus's lips raised slightly in a smile, as he turned to look at Leia.

"What's wrong, Leia?" he asked. "You look different. Is something the matter?"

Instantly, the Human Replica Droid's eyes

glowed bright green, as piercing laser beams shot out of them, meeting at a fiery, sizzling point.

ZZZZZZZZCH!

The lasers burned a hole in Trioculus's chest.

"Ahhhhhhh! Demon of darknesssss . . . . " Trioculus cried. He curled up on the floor, as blood began to flow with every beat of his heart.

THUMP . . . THUMP . . . THUMP . . . .

The grand moffs and those who had gathered were aghast at their leader's fate.

Grand Moff Hissa, furiously gnashing his spiked teeth, dropped the Dark Book of Imperial Justice and raised his laser pistol. He fired at Leia again and again without stopping.

The Human Replica Droid fell to the floor alongside Trioculus.

Hissa gasped as he saw the artificial skin melting from Leia's face, revealing her mechanized circuitry. The Leia whom Trioculus was about to marry was only a droid, he realized. The Rebel Alliance had deceived them once again.

Inside the *Millennium Falcon*, Han Solo and Princess Leia embraced.

"*Chnooch-tzeepch!*" Artoo-Detoo beeped.

"Artoo is sorry to have to break up your party," See-Threepio translated, "but we're still fastened to the top of the Moffship, and that's hardly an appropriate place for a celebration."

"I have to agree with Threepio," Luke said, turning to Ken and Lando, with a wink.

Taking their hint, Han turned his attention to the navigation panel and demonstrated his well-established skills and expertise in interstellar piloting.

Within just a few short moments, the *Falcon* was flying away as fast as its sublight thrusters could carry it, soaring through the upper atmosphere of Tatooine and far from the Moffship. As soon as it reached the threshold of space, Han activated the hyperdrive unit, sending the *Falcon* on a hasty departure at faster-than-light speed.

"Maybe eloping wasn't such a great idea," Han said, adjusting the dials on his navigation console. "Maybe having a more formal wedding would have been a better plan."

"I don't mind the delay," Leia replied. "Now we'll be able to invite Luke and Lando and Ken and Baji and Mon Mothma and Chewie—"

"Whoa there," Han interrupted. "How extravagant are these nuptials going to be, anyway? I thought we agreed—simple, quick, quiet . . . painless."

"My brother Luke should be there to give away the bride, don't you agree?" Leia shot back.

"And Chewie should certainly be there as your best man, Han," Lando added.

"Except for the fact that he isn't a man," Han argued, nitpicking over the subtle point. "He's a Wookiee."

"I never heard of any law that says a Wookiee can't be the best man," Luke interjected.

"*ChnooOOch-gzEEch!*" Artoo tooted.

"What are *you* fussing about, Artoo?" See-Threepio demanded impatiently.

"*BzeeEEEk-zpooook!*"

"No, you *can't* be the best droid at the wedding," Threepio replied. "For one thing, there's no such thing, so you have a lot of nerve even suggesting it. And if there *were* such a thing as a best droid, I'm quite sure Princess Leia would decide to reserve that position of honor for *me*!"

As Emdee-Five and a team of Imperial medical droids struggled to save Trioculus's fading life, the Moffship departed from Tatooine and the region of the Great Pit of Carkoon, soaring into space.

Meanwhile, down in the pit, the Mouth of Sarlacc stirred.

No one was there to see or hear it, but the mouth coughed and choked, then belched and burped.

In a terrible fit of indigestion, it spit out Zorba the

Hutt, heaving him up with such incredible force, that Zorba landed on the sand outside the pit, on solid ground.

Zorba wiggled and shook and brushed the sticky stomach juices off his blubbery body.

"Well, I didn't care for the taste of you, *either*!" Zorba exclaimed. "You should know better than to try to swallow a Hutt! No creature in the galaxy can digest us—not even you!"

And then Zorba's roaring laugh bellowed out across the sandy plain—a laugh that only he and the Sarlacc could hear.

"A-HAW-HAW-HAWWWWW . . . . . . !"

To find out what happens when Zorba the Hutt joins forces with Kadann, the Supreme Prophet of the Dark Side, don't miss *Prophets of the Dark Side*, book six of our continuing Star Wars adventures.

Here's a preview:

The tubular transport started to vibrate furiously, and then it slowed to a dead stop halfway up the elevator shaft.

The power had failed. They were trapped.

"Uh-oh," Ken said despondently. "Looks like we're history."

"Aren't you forgetting something, Ken?" Luke Skywalker asked, putting a hand on the young Jedi Prince's shoulder.

"Like what?"

"The Force. With trust in the Force, we can do *anything*," Luke said. "Even move tons of solid steel. Once I watched Yoda use the Force to lift my spaceship out of the swamps of Dagobah—it floated, weightless, until he set it down. The Force is a Jedi's strength, Ken. The Force is the power behind the light of the stars—"

In the darkness, Luke began to banish all other thoughts from his mind, putting himself in harmony with the Force, letting its power and energy flow through him. He breathed slowly, evenly, forgetting about the rising and falling of his chest, the inhales, the exhales. Only one thought remained in his mind—

the wonder of the Force.

Suddenly there was a brief jolt, and the transport rose several inches. A few seconds passed. Then came a slow, gliding movement upward, as the power of the Force helped the transport move several feet farther. There was about a mile left to go.

"Help me, Ken," Luke said. "Empty your mind . . . feel the Force."

Ken tried to banish his fears and all other thoughts from his mind. He knew that this tubular transport was like a deep underground coffin. If it never moved again, the transport would become their tomb—in a million years, some explorer might find this elevator shaft and discover their remains.

But Ken knew he had to have positive thoughts— thoughts of life, not death.

"Only the Force, Ken," Luke said. "Keep your whole mind, your entire being focused on the Force."

Suddenly the tubular transport began to move. It ascended slowly at first, and then it accelerated, going faster and faster as it continued to rise inside the elevator shaft—powered only by the pure energy of the Force.

Will Ken betray the droids of the Lost City of the Jedi who raised him, so he can discover the identity of his father? And will Ken do the bidding of Kadann, the Supreme Prophet of the Dark Side, in the hopes that the Empire will spare Luke Skywalker's life? Find out in *Prophets of the Dark Side*, coming soon.

Glossary

Audit Droids
Droids such as Checksum and his assistant Debit-101, a specialist in business strategies.

Baji
A Ho'Din alien, a healer and medicine man whom Luke met in the rain forest on the fourth moon of Yavin. After being captured by the Empire and forced to cure Trioculus's blindness, Baji was kept on as an Imperial staff physician, but was later rescued by the Rebel Alliance. He now lives a simple life at DRAPAC on Dagobah, tending to his medicinal plants in the Alliance's greenhouse.

Bithabus the Mystifier
An alien of the Bith species. Bithabus is a performing stage magician famous throughout the galaxy, who does a regular magic show at the Asteroid Theater at Hologram Fun World.

Boulder-Dozer
Similar to a bulldozer in overall design, a Boulder-Dozer is equipped with laser-scorchers that are capable of vaporizing rock or other types of heavy debris. The best ones are made by the Rendili Vehicle Corporation, a Corellian company, and are equipped with Navicomputer controls.

Cobak
An alien of the Bith species, Cobak is a bounty hunter hired by Zorba the Hutt. He impersonates Bithabus the Mystifier at the Asteroid Theater at Hologram Fun World, in a plot to capture Princess Leia.

Carbonite
A substance made from Tibanna gas, plentiful on the planet Bespin, where it is mined and sold in liquid form as a fuel in Cloud City. When carbonite is turned into a solid, it can be used for keeping humans or other organisms alive in a state of suspended animation, encasing them completely.

Chad
A civilized and beautiful planet where the Chadra-Fan aliens live. Chad has rolling hills and willowy cyperil trees overlooking fields where Lactils graze by the millions. Lactils are a breed of alien milk-producing cows that support Chad's extensive dairy industry.

Chadra-Fan
Small, quick-witted creatures from the planet Chad, resembling rodents. Chadra-Fan have large, flappy ears, dark eyes, and a flattened circular nose with four nostrils. Their combination of infrared sight, hypersensitive sense of smell, and keen hearing help make the Chadra-Fan physically and mentally perceptive creatures.

Cloud City
A floating city above the planet Bespin that used to be a popular center of tourism, with its hotels and casinos. It is considered one of the galaxy's major trading posts, and the site of a Tibanna gas mining and exporting operation.

DRAPAC
Acronym for the Defense Research and Planetary Assistance Center, a Rebel Alliance fortress built at the peak of Mount Yoda on the planet Dagobah. The secret Alliance group called SPIN—the Senate Planetary Intelligence

Network—moved its central offices from Yavin Four and relocated them to DRAPAC, after Trioculus invaded the fourth moon of Yavin during his search for the Lost City of the Jedi.

Fandar
A brilliant Chadra-Fan scientist, credited with managing Project Decoy—the creation of a lifelike Human Replica Droid, the prototype of which resembles Princess Leia.

Fugo
Fandar's scientific colleague, also of the Chadra-Fan species. When Fandar is injured and cannot continue with Project Decoy, Fugo carries on in Fandar's absence.

Hologram Fun World
Located inside a glowing, transparent dome floating in the center of a blue cloud of helium gas in outer space, Hologram Fun World is a theme park, where a "World of Dreams Come True" awaits every vistor. Lando Calrissian is now the Baron Administrator of the theme park.

Human Replica Droid
A lifelike droid designed to look like a specific person. Its purpose is to act as a decoy and fool an enemy into thinking it's real. Designed by the Chadra-Fan alien scientists, Fandar and Fugo, in a secret Rebel Alliance lab at DRAPAC, Human Replica Droids have eyes that can fire laser beams.

Jabba the Hutt
A sluglike alien gangster and smuggler who owned a palace on Tatooine and consorted with alien bounty hunters. He was strangled to death by Princess Leia, choked by

the chain that held her prisoner in his sail barge at the Great Pit of Carkoon.

Ken

A twelve-year-old Jedi prince, who was raised by droids in the Lost City of the Jedi. He was brought to the underground city as a small child by a Jedi Knight in a brown robe. He knows nothing of his origins, but he does know many Imperial secrets, which he learned from studying the files of the master Jedi computer in the Jedi Library where he went to school. Long an admirer of Luke Skywalker, he has departed the Lost City and joined the Alliance.

Kowakian monkey-lizard

A rare species of the planet Kowak, monkey-lizards are famous for their silliness and stupidity. Just as people of our day call someone a "monkey's uncle" as a snide remark, in the Star Wars universe it's an insult to be called a Kowakian monkey-lizard.

Lactil

A breed of milk-producing alien cow that is the basis of the dairy industry of the planet Chad.

Lando Calrissian

A friend of Han Solo who gambled away the *Millennium Falcon* to Han in a friendly game of sabacc. Lando used to be Governor and Baron Administrator of Cloud City on the planet Bespin. After losing his position to Zorba the Hutt, Lando is now Baron Administrator of Hologram Fun World.

Lost City of the Jedi

An ancient, technologically advanced city built long ago

by Jedi Knights. The city is located deep underground on the fourth moon of Yavin, where Ken, the Jedi Prince, was raised by droids.

Mouth of Sarlacc
A giant, omnivorous, multitentacled beast at the bottom of the Great Pit of Carkoon on Tatooine, beyond the Dune Sea. Anyone who falls to the bottom of the pit will be swallowed by the Sarlacc and slowly digested over a period of one thousand years.

Project Decoy
The secret Alliance project for making Human Replica Droids.

Shutter-Bug-9 (SB-9)
A picture-taking droid photographer at Hologram Fun World who Lando assigns to take pictures for Han and Leia's wedding album. SB-9 has a camera built into his chest, and his eyes are strobe lights that flash whenever he snaps a picture.

SPIN
An acronym for the Senate Planetary Intelligence Network, a Rebel Alliance troubleshooting organization. All the major Star Wars Alliance heroes are members of SPIN, which has offices both on Yavin Four and at DRAPAC on Mount Yoda on the planet Dagobah.

Triclops
The true son of the evil Emperor Palpatine. Triclops is a mutant, with a third eye in the back of his head. For most of his life, Triclops was imprisoned in Imperial insane asylums, under the authority of Trioculus, the former

Supreme Slavelord of Kessel. Triclops later escaped from the Imperial Reprogramming Institute on the planet Duro. Luke Skywalker and Ken found him and brought him back to DRAPAC. Shrouded in mystery, the Empire considers Triclops insane and fears disaster if he were ever to become Emperor, like his father. Triclops claims he believes in peace and disarming his father's evil Empire, but he may in fact be a brilliant madman with a split personality. When he sleeps, Triclops invents terrible weapons of destruction in his dreams.

Trioculus
Like Triclops, Trioculus also has three eyes, but all of his are on the front of his face. With the help of the grand moffs, Trioculus rose from the position of Supreme Slavelord of the spice mines of Kessel to become the new Emperor of the Galactic Empire after the death of the evil Emperor Palpatine. Trioculus is an impostor, not a true master of the Dark Side, and falsely claims to be Emperor Palpatine's real three-eyed son. He wears on his hand a duplicate of the glove of Darth Vader, an everlasting symbol of evil.

Zinthorn flowers
Black flowers used for Imperial wedding bouquets.

Zorba the Hutt
The father of Jabba the Hutt. A sluglike creature with a long braided white beard, Zorba was a prisoner on the planet Kip for over twenty years. He returned to Tatooine to discover that his son was killed by Princess Leia. He later became Governor of Cloud City by beating Lando Calrissian in a rigged card game of sabacc in the Holiday Towers Hotel and Casino.

PAUL DAVIDS, a graduate of Princeton University and the American Film Institute Center for Advanced Film Studies, has had a lifelong love of science fiction. He was the executive producer of and cowrote the film *Roswell* for Showtime. *Roswell* starred Kyle MacLachlan and Martin Sheen and was nominated for a Golden Globe for Best TV Motion Picture of 1994.

Paul was the production coordinator and a writer for the television series *The Transformers*. He is currently the producer and director of a documentary feature film titled *Timothy Leary's Dead*. His first book, *The Fires of Pele: Mark Twain's Legendary Lost Journal*, was written with his wife, Hollace, with whom he also wrote the six Skylark Star Wars novels. The Davids live in Los Angeles.

HOLLACE DAVIDS is Vice President of Special Projects at Universal Pictures. Her job includes planning and coordinating all the studio's premieres and working on the Academy Awards campaigns. Hollace has an A.B. in psychology, *cum laude*, from Goucher College and an Ed.M. in counseling psychology from Boston University. After teaching children with learning disabilities, Hollace began her career in the entertainment business by working for the Los Angeles International Film Exposition. She then became a publicist at Columbia Pictures, and seven years later was named Vice President of Special Projects at Columbia. She has also worked for TriStar Pictures and Sony Pictures Entertainment.

Whether it's because they grew up in nearby hometowns (Hollace is from Silver Spring, Maryland, and Paul is from Bethesda) or because they share many interests, collaboration comes naturally to Paul and Hollace Davids—both in their writing and in raising a family. The Davids have a daughter, Jordan, and a son, Scott.

About the Illustrators

JUNE BRIGMAN was born in 1960 in Atlanta, Georgia, and has been drawing since she was old enough to hold a pencil. She studied art at the University of Georgia and Georgia State University, but her illustrations are based on real-life observation and skills she developed over a summer as a pastel portrait artist at Six Flags Over Georgia amusement park, when she was only sixteen. At twenty she discovered comic books at a comic convention, and by the time she was twenty-two she got her first job working for Marvel Comics, where she created the *Power Pack* series. A devout horse enthusiast and Bruce Springsteen fan, Ms. Brigman lives and works in White Plains, New York.

KARL KESEL was born in 1959 and raised in the small town of Victor, New York. He started reading comic books at the age of ten, while traveling cross-country with his family, and decided soon after that he wanted to become a cartoonist. By the age of twenty-five, he landed a full-time job as an illustrator for DC Comics, working on such titles as *Superman*, *World's Finest*, *Newsboy Legion*, and *Hawk and Dove*, which he also cowrote. He was also one of the artists on the *Terminator* and *Indiana Jones* miniseries for Dark Horse Comics. Mr. Kesel lives and works with his wife, Barbara, in Milwaukie, Oregon.

DREW STRUZAN is a teacher, lecturer, and one of the most influential forces working in commercial art today. His strong visual sense and recognizable style have produced lasting pieces of art for advertising, the recording industry, and motion pictures. His paintings include the album covers for *Alice Cooper's Greatest Hits* and *Welcome to My Nightmare*, which was recently voted one of the one hundred classic album covers of all time by *Rolling Stone* magazine. He has also created the movie posters for Star Wars, *E.T. the Extra-Terrestrial*, the Back to the Future series, the Indiana Jones series, *An American Tale*, and *Hook*. Mr. Struzan lives and works in the California valley with his wife, Cheryle. Their son, Christian, is continuing in the family tradition, working as an art director and illustrator.

In A Galaxy Far, Far Away

In the Heart of the Empire

A New Evil Lurks . . .

STAR WARS®
GALAXY of FEAR

Don't miss book #1, <u>Eaten Alive</u>, in this spine-chilling new series, featuring an exclusive limited edition hologram cover!

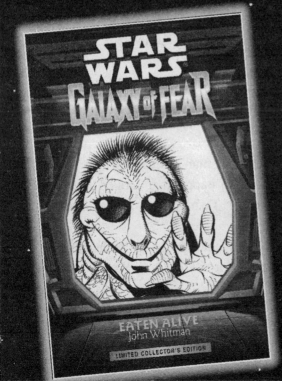

On sale now at a galaxy or bookstore near you.

Turn the page for a sneak peek.

BFYR 141

In this excerpt from Star Wars: Galaxy of Fear #1, *Eaten Alive,* Tash and Zak Arranda and their uncle Hoole are stranded on a strange and mysterious planet where nothing is as it seems. . . .

Suddenly a tall man stepped out of the shadows, pointing a well-worn blaster at Smada. "I don't think so," he said.

"This is none of your concern, stranger," Smada growled.

The tall man answered with a cocky grin. "I'm making it my business."

"And mine," said a young woman, who appeared beside the man.

"And mine," said another man with blond hair. He ignited a strange, glowing weapon that looked like a sword made of pure energy. Tash gasped. A Jedi *lightsaber*!

"And his," said the tall man, pointing to the huge Wookiee Tash had seen before. The furry Wookiee let out a threatening roar.

If looks had been lasers, Smada would have inciner-
ated them all. But he obviously didn't want to fight.
"D'vouran is a small planet, Hoole. We'll meet again."

Smada signaled to his thugs, who freed Zak and
Tash. Tash saw that Smada had been sitting on a hover-
sled, a long platform that floated in the air. With his
bodyguards around him, Smada the Hutt floated out of
the cantina. Since there was nothing left to watch, the
rest of the cantina patrons went back to their business,
and the noise resumed.

The tall man and the woman holstered their blasters,
while the blond man deactivated his lightsaber. Behind
them hovered two droids, a stocky R2 unit and a golden
protocol droid.

"Oh, what a relief! I was about to short circuit!" the
droid said. "Shouldn't we notify the authorities?"

"Pipe down, Threepio," the tall man said. "There
aren't any authorities on D'vouran. Just the Enzeen, and
they're too friendly to do much about Smada." He
looked at Hoole. "Everyone okay?"

"Yes," Hoole said. "Luckily Smada was more interested in making threats than hurting anyone. Thank you
for your help."

"What was that all about?" Tash asked her uncle.

"He seemed to know you," the young man with the
lightsaber observed.

Hoole hesitated. Finally he said cautiously, "Yes. He

. . . offered me a job several years ago. When I refused to accept, he swore that he would have his revenge. It was a coincidence that brought us together on this planet.''

"An unhappy one, I'd say," the woman added. "That Smada's pretty foul-tempered, even for a Hutt."

"I've known worse," the tall man said.

The Shi'ido introduced himself. "My name is Hoole."

"I'm Han Solo. Call me Han," said the tall man. He had the casual confidence of a starpilot. "This is my partner, Chewbacca," he added, indicating the Wookiee. Then he pointed at the woman. "And this is—"

"Princess Leia," Tash finished.

The woman blinked. All the newcomers looked around to make sure no one had overheard. Han Solo's hand crept toward the blastor slung low on his hip.

The young man with the lightsaber saw the movement and said, "It's all right, Han."

But Han growled, "I'm not taking any chances."

The woman, Leia, gently put her hand over Han's. "Let me handle this." To Tash, she said, "What makes you think that's my name?"

Zak shook his head. "It's gotta be. Tash is always right about stuff like that. It's weird."

Tash said, "It's not so weird! Zak and I live on Alderaan, where you're from. I mean, we did . . . before it . . . well, you know.''

She could see from the woman's face that Leia knew very well what had happened to Alderaan.

Beside her, Zak almost shouted, ''Hey, are you guys *Rebels?*''

''Zak!'' Tash hissed.

Han's face turned to a scowl. ''We're minding our own business, kid, which is what you should be doing.''

''We're . . . researchers,'' Leia interrupted gently. ''We're looking this planet over for some friends of ours. We were just about to leave, but we couldn't sit back and let that Hutt threaten you.''

Tash heard Uncle Hoole reply, ''I am a researcher, too.'' But she remembered the Hutt's words: *There's a lot about your uncle that you don't know.*

There's a lot about everyone *I don't know,* Tash thought. Leia had been a princess on Alderaan. Whatever she was doing with these people was a lot more important than ''research.''

''Maybe,'' Tash said hesitantly, ''we could sit down for a while. You could tell us about your *research—*''

''Of course we will,'' Leia interrupted with a quick glance at Han. ''We'll stay at least until we're sure that Hutt doesn't come back around.''

The two parties sat down together. Han Solo propped his feet up on an empty chair. ''Order anything you want. The food's free you know. These Enzeen will feed you till you're ready to burst.''

Uncle Hoole nodded. ''We've only met one, but he seems extremely friendly.''

To Zak's delight, they did order food from a passing waiter. Moments later the Enzeen reappeared with plates piled high with all sorts of exotic meats, pastries, and fruits. Zak wrinkled his nose at a dish full of eight-legged insects covered in a pink sauce. But when he dipped a finger into the sauce and tasted it, his eyes lit up and he began shoveling it in. The only one at the table who kept up with him was the Wookiee.

Tash had no appetite. Her stomach was in a knot—the feeling of fear had not gone away. She was trying to ignore it. It was probably just her imagination anyway, and she refused to make a fool of herself the way she'd done when the Enzeen put the flowers around her neck.

As they began to eat, everyone relaxed. Even Han Solo seemed to be interested as Uncle Hoole and Zak described their journey. But Tash drifted from one conversation to another, unable to concentrate. Deevee had been cornered by C-3PO and his companion, R2-D2.

''. . . and then I found myself alone on the planet Tatooine, wandering through that terrible desert!'' Threepio was saying. ''It was perfectly dreadful.''

"Fascinating, I'm sure," Deevee replied. He looked as bored as a droid could look.

"Wait until you hear what happened next!" Threepio trilled.

"I don't suppose you were deactivated or anything convenient like that?" Deevee asked.

"Well, no."

"Too bad," the unhappy droid muttered. "Well, you might as well go on, then, . . ."

Tash could barely pay attention. Maybe it was the exotic food, or maybe the feeling of being watched was growing stronger, but she thought she might be sick. The sensation was so strong that she had actually forgotten about the blond man with the Jedi lightsaber, until he leaned across the table to speak to her.

"Is everything all right?" he asked.

"Um, yeah. Fine," she said.

The young man smiled. "Your name's Tash, right? I'm Luke. Luke Skywalker."

Something about him made her feel strange. Not "strange" like the crushes she'd had on boys back on Alderaan—she had outgrown crushes anyway. This was a sense of . . . relief. Tash felt as if she'd been waiting to meet someone like Luke Skywalker all her life.

His blue eyes stared at her like a scanner reaching into her deepest thoughts. "Something's troubling you."

"I guess," Tash began. She never liked telling people about the feelings she sometimes got. But she found herself confiding in him easily. "I guess I feel a little uneasy here. I don't know what exactly, but something's bothering me. It's probably just my imagination." She didn't expect him to understand, since no one ever understood.

To her surprise, Luke said, "Not too long ago, a good friend taught me a very important lesson: trust your feelings."

From the next chair, Chewbacca barked a question at Hoole, and Han translated. "So you say you dropped out of hyperspace fifteen minutes too early?"

"Uncle Hoole nodded. "It caused a great deal of damage to our ship."

"The same thing happened to us. My ship, the *Millennium Falcon,* got shaken up pretty good." The starpilot shook his head. "I don't know, maybe it's just an error in the star charts."

"Perhaps," Uncle Hoole agreed. "But in our case, I think it was some problems we had on board." He glared at Tash.

Zak laughed. "He means Tash. She was playing Jedi Knight in the cockpit."

Tash felt her face grow red. Luke Skywalker raised an eyebrow and gave her a knowing smile. "So you want to be a Jedi, do you?"

"I've read about them," she confessed. "My parents were on Alderaan when it . . . you know. I always thought that if there were more Jedi, they wouldn't have let it happen."

"They do their best, Tash," Luke said. "That's all any of us can do."

"Are—are you a Jedi?" she asked almost in a whisper, pointing at his lightsaber.

Luke shook his head. "I wish I could say yes. But no, I'm not. This lightsaber belonged to my father."

Tash nodded sadly. "They say all the Jedi are gone now. So I don't know how I'd ever find one to teach me."

Luke put his hand on her shoulder. He whispered, "Don't give up hope yet. You might be surprised. A Jedi might come looking for you someday."

Tash wanted to know what he meant by that. But she didn't get a chance to ask. Because at that moment, someone screamed.

The scream came from outside, somewhere near the cantina. Most of the patrons looked up just long enough to make sure they were in no danger, then ignored the cries. They had come to this new planet to escape trouble, not to find it.

But everyone at Tash's table jumped up and ran toward the door. The cries were coming from behind the cantina. Their new friends—Tash was now sure they were Rebels, because they acted with so much courage—drew their weapons.

But the street was deserted except for the wild man, Bebo. He was on his knees, scratching at the dirt and shouting. "No! No! No!"

Tash was not afraid of Bebo. "What's wrong?" she asked him.

"She's gone! She's gone!" the madman croaked. "My friend Lonni was standing here a minute ago, and she just vanished!"

"What do you mean 'vanished'?" Hoole asked.

Bebo stood up. The light in his eyes had become fierce. "I mean vanished! Gone! Disappeared! And it's all my fault! I convinced her to come out of hiding. To warn everyone! They didn't believe me, but they might believe her. She came because I told her she'd be safe! But she's gone. She was standing here, and then she wasn't!"

Although no one from the cantina had come out, a few settlers had come to investigate the shouting. These people were a more wholesome-looking crowd, Tash noted. Probably the families and pioneers Chood had mentioned. But they seemed as uninterested in Bebo's ravings as the cantina patrons. In fact, most of them were laughing.

Someone called out, "Go ahead, Bebo! Tell us another!"

"Yeah," someone added, "Tell us about vanishing people!"

"And invisible monsters!"

"Or was it invisible people and vanishing monsters?"

The crowd laughed at the joke. Chood appeared, and for a split second, Tash thought she saw the smile leave his face at the sight of Bebo. But it reappeared again, as bright as ever. "May I be of service?"

Tash pointed to Bebo. "He needs help. A friend of his disappeared."

Chood sighed. "I'm sorry if this has troubled anyone. Unfortunately Bebo has done this many times before. I assure you that no one has disappeared."

"Lonni disappeared!" Bebo's voice dropped into a whisper. "She was my only friend."

Tash felt something tug at her heart. She knew what it was like to lose someone.

One of the settlers called out, "You're crazy, Bebo!"

Chood nodded. "Sadly, it's true. Ever since he came here, poor Bebo has been ranting and raving about disappearances."

"It's true!" Bebo responded. "They died. The entire crew of the *Misanthrope*! They disappeared!"

Chood gazed sympathetically at Bebo, then turned to Hoole and the others and said softly, "This is a sad tale. The *Misanthrope* was the cargo ship that first crashed here. Bebo, here, was the captain and the only survivor. I'm afraid the guilt was too much for his mind. It snapped."

"No, no, no!" Bebo argued. "They disappeared. All of them!"

"He should be treated at a mental facility," observed Deevee.

"It's not that simple," Chood replied. "The official report said that he was responsible for the crash. If he leaves the planet, he'll be thrown into prison. But we Enzeen are a little more sympathetic, so we let him live here, despite the fact that he continually disrupts the environment we try to create for our settlers."

"Have you followed up on his claims that there were other survivors?" Hoole asked. "Who is this Lonni person he talks of?"

"There was a full investigation of the crash," the Enzeen replied. "And the Imperial officials declared no survivors. This person Bebo is raving about could not have lived."

"That's a lie!" Bebo snapped. "She was here!"

"Oh, really?" Chood said. His voice was still very calm and pleasant. "Then, please tell me, Bebo, where was your friend when she disappeared?"

Bebo pointed at the ground. "Right there! Right there! We were walking along, and *poof!* she was gone!"

"Walking along, you say? Are those your footprints, then?" Chood pointed at a line of footprints in the dirt road.

"Yes! That's where I was."

"Then where are your friend's footprints?" the Enzeen asked.

"Why they're right . . ." For the first time, Bebo stopped muttering to himself. There were no other footprints on the ground. There was no sign that anyone but Bebo had been standing there. "But she was right there! Right there!"

Chood shrugged. "You see. He is quite mad. It is most regrettable."

"Can't you help him? At least search the village?" Tash asked.

"We can, but we won't find anything," Chood said. "People who wish to be found on D'vouran are easy to find. Those who wish to hide, well, it's a large planet."

By this time, most of the settlers had lost interest and gone about their business. Uncle Hoole, too, wanted to move on. "Let's go, Tash," he said. "These people have offered to help us fix the *Lightrunner,* and we can't keep them waiting.''

As the others turned away, Tash said softly to Bebo, ''I'm sorry I can't help you. I wish there was something I could do for you.''

Bebo gave her a cold, hard look. ''It doesn't matter. Before long you'll be dead. You're all going to die.''